Take time out from yo... ...onth to
kick back and relax wi... ...arlequin Presents
novel. We hope you enjo... ...onth's selection.

If you love royal heroes, you're in for a treat this month!
In Penny Jordan's latest book, *The Italian Duke's Wife*,
an Italian aristocrat chooses a young English woman
as his convenient wife. When he unleashes within
her a desire she never knew she possessed, he is soon
regretting his no-consummation rule.... Emma Darcy's
sheikh in *Traded to the Sheikh* is an equally powerful
and sexy alpha male. This story has a wonderfully exotic
desert setting, too!

We have some gorgeous European men this month.
Shackled by Diamonds by Julia James is part of our
popular miniseries GREEK TYCOONS. Read about a
Greek tycoon and the revenge he plans to exact on an
innocent, beautiful model when he wrongly suspects
her of stealing his priceless diamonds. In Sarah Morgan's
Public Wife, Private Mistress, can a passionate Italian's
marriage be rekindled when he is unexpectedly reunited
with his estranged wife?

In *The Antonides Marriage Deal* by Anne McAllister, a
Greek magnate meets a stunning new business partner,
and he begins to wonder if he can turn their business
arrangement into a permanent contract—such as
marriage! Kay Thorpe's *Bought by a Billionaire* tells of
a Portuguese billionaire and his ex-lover. He wants her
back as his mistress. Previously she rejected his proposal
because of his arrogance and his powerful sexuality. But
this time he wants marriage....

Happy reading! Look out for a brand-new selection next
month.

Cathy Williams

THE RICH MAN'S MISTRESS

TORONTO • NEW YORK • LONDON
AMSTERDAM • PARIS • SYDNEY • HAMBURG
STOCKHOLM • ATHENS • TOKYO • MILAN • MADRID
PRAGUE • WARSAW • BUDAPEST • AUCKLAND

ISBN 0-373-18872-2

THE RICH MAN'S MISTRESS

First North American Publication 2006.

Copyright © 2002 by Cathy Williams.

This edition published by arrangement with Harlequin Books S.A.

® and TM are trademarks of the publisher. Trademarks indicated with
® are registered in the United States Patent and Trademark Office, the
Canadian Trade Marks Office and in other countries.

www.eHarlequin.com

Printed in U.S.A.

All about the author...
Cathy Williams

CATHY WILLIAMS was born in the West Indies and has been writing for the Harlequin Presents line for over fifteen years. She is a great believer in the power of perseverance as she had never written anything before and from the starting point of zero has now fulfilled her ambition to pursue this most enjoyable of careers. She would encourage any would-be writer to have faith and go for it!

She lives in the beautiful Warwickshire countryside with her husband and three children, Charlotte, Olivia and Emma. When not writing she is hard-pressed to find a moment's free time in between the millions of household chores, not to mention being a one-woman taxi service for her daughters' never-ending social lives.

She derives inspiration from the hot, lazy, tropical island of Trinidad (where she was born), from the peaceful countryside of middle England and, of course, from her many friends, who are a rich source of plots and are particularly garrulous when it comes to describing her heroes. It would seem from their complaints that tall, dark and charismatic men are too few and far between! Her hope is to continue writing romance fiction and providing those eternal tales of love for which, she feels, we all strive.

CHAPTER ONE

MIRANDA paused and looked behind her, then she slowly turned a full circle. This was a big mistake because the slow beat of panic which had been curling inside her stomach for the past hour mushroomed into full-blown fear as she was forced to contemplate her complete isolation. She had no idea where she was. She had no idea where she was going. All sense of direction had been lost as she had skied rapidly away from the avalanche straight into a blizzard that was now making forward progress laborious and uncertain. And, to make matters worse, dusk was beginning to permeate the great white amphitheatre which had always seemed so gloriously free and now appeared terrifyingly hostile.

She whimpered and found that she was having to make an effort to remind herself that she was an expert skier, had been doing it for twenty-two of her twenty-five years. She could more than handle the challenge of the black runs. With the snow whipping like pellets against the parts of her face which were exposed, and restricting any clear view that might help her to get her bearings, she would have to move slowly and keep her fingers crossed that she was going in the right direction.

Anger gave way to self-pity and she skied slowly towards a small cluster of fir trees which offered the only visual relief from the naked, virgin-white landscape, barely visible now as the light continued to fade.

She was lost, alone, terrified and quite possibly on course for a date with the Grim Reaper, and all because

Freddie, her so-called boyfriend, couldn't keep his immature, wandering hands to himself. Not content with having had her there with him, he'd simply had to explore the voluptuous charm of the Italian eighteen-year-old girl who had been assigned to their chalet. And worse, had got caught doing it.

How dared he?

Miranda leaned against the trunk of a tree and closed her eyes. She had to take a few deep breaths to contain her rage or else she would scream at the top of her lungs and, with her luck, probably set off another avalanche. Her woollen hat was soaked from the snow. She should never have worn it. She should have stuck on her faithful, waterproof headgear instead of a flimsy hat simply because it matched the rest of her skiing outfit. Now she could feel the dampness permeating through to her head. As far as everything else was concerned, she was well-protected with all the requisite layers of clothing, including thick, waterproof gloves. But how long would she be able to remain stationary before the cold began sinking its teeth through the layers in search of flesh? She squinted into the dying light and dimly made out a thickish cluster of trees, a dense little patch that would be more protection for her should an overnight stay outdoors become necessary.

Miranda groaned. Why kid herself that she was miraculously going to find her way back to the chalet where Freddie and their fifteen-strong group were right now probably cracking open their first bottle and contemplating what to have for supper? Would they even have missed her? Or, if they had, would they have assumed that she was miserably lost and perilously close to despair in the middle of nowhereland? They were all first-class skiers and they would probably be unaware of the minor avalanche that had thrown her so badly off course. Doubtless Freddie would have made a story about their argument, reducing his despicable behaviour to the level of some boyish jollity that had been misconstrued by a jealous girlfriend and her absence would be put down to a minor blip. Quite possibly they would assume that she had needed to cool off and had taken herself off to one of the hotels in a huff. Her platinum credit card would have gained her entry into any of the hotels further down the slope if she felt she needed time out and they all knew that she travelled with it in her inside jacket pocket.

'Just in case a fabulous shop happens to beckon unexpectedly!' she had always joked.

Fat lot of good a credit card was going to do for her now.

She wearily adjusted her skies and headed towards the vanishing clump of trees, moving at a snail's pace down the steep slope, making sure that desperation didn't propel her to do anything stupid. With luck, the trees would block out the blizzard or at least keep it at bay and, if she huddled into a ball in the centre of them, she might just be able to last out the night. With even greater luck she might find shelter in one of the animal sheds that were dotted around here and there but she wouldn't let any optimism blind her to the stark reality that she might just find more trees.

The vast white terrain was now almost completely swamped in darkness. If she hadn't been so focused on making it to the trees while she could still see them, she might not have stumbled and fallen over the projecting stump, rolling powerlessly down the slope. One of her skies dislodged automatically, the other clung to her foot; and when she finally came to a slow halt and tried to stand, the pain shot through her ankle like an explosion.

The lost ski, which would be essential for her to get out of this mess, was nowhere to be seen. The fast-falling snow had buried it like a matchstick and there was no time to instigate a hunt.

Miranda felt panic turn her bones to water and she gritted her teeth, forcing herself down the last few metres towards the trees, dragging her useless foot and using her ski poles like crutches.

She had been right. The blizzard, at least, was kept at bay by the denseness of the trees. She forced herself forward and was about to pause for a rest when she saw a flicker of light. When she angled her body for a better view, the light disappeared; but then, back in the original position, it reappeared. Something bright through the trees.

She could feel her eyes getting heavy and made herself stand back up, lifting her damaged leg as though she was just about to begin a game of hopscotch. The pain was excruciating, but far less so when there was no weight applied.

If she ever made it back home in one piece, then she would turn her life around. No more flitting from one fun spot to another in search of thrills. No more frantic social life—paid for by her wealthy daddy—in the company of other young, rich, restless friends from similarly wealthy backgrounds. And no more Freddie. That went without saying. In fact no more men. And definitely no more rich, spoiled brats.

The light was getting more constant now.

Miranda was virtually crying from the anticipation of finding it. The trees had become shapeless black towers and she had to weave her way painfully around them until, without warning, they cleared and the source of the light became apparent.

Not an animal shed but a cabin. Fairly small, with the typically pointed roof and, more importantly, inhabited. The curtains were drawn against the darkness but the light inside promised occupation. Help. She gave a deep-throated sob and dragged her way to the door, collapsing in exhaustion after one loud bang.

Which meant that her first view of her rescuer, her saviour, was of his feet. Or rather of his brown, weathered loafers. When he spoke his voice seemed to come from a long way off. A nice voice, she thought distractedly, deep. She lacked the energy to raise her head to inspect the face that went with the voice. She closed her eyes on a sigh and felt him lift her up and carry her into the blissful warmth of the cabin, kicking shut the door behind him.

It felt unbelievably good to be out of the cold. So good, in fact, that she wondered whether she was dreaming and whether, in a minute, she would open her eyes only to find that she was huddled under a tree fending off the same blizzard and any hopes of rescue, cabins, flickering lights and warmth were the delusions of a wandering mind.

Which was why she kept her eyes closed as she was deposited gently on a sofa that felt broad and comfortable enough to be a bed.

'Who,' the voice said from above her, 'the hell are you and what are you doing here?'

Less of a question and more of a demand for an immediate explanation. Miranda opened her eyes and found herself staring upwards at the harsh angles of an aggressively dominant face and at narrowed cobalt-blue eyes that were staring back at her with a mixture of suspicion and hostility.

He was wearing a baggy and very faded dark blue and white striped tee shirt and a pair of loose grey jogging pants that, like the shirt, seemed to have seen better days many moons before.

She forgot the pain in the ankle in the face of this overwhelming show of rudeness.

Never before in her life had any man ever reacted to her like this before! True, she probably wasn't looking her best right at this very moment, but still. She felt her mouth droop into a petulant scowl which only made her unwelcome saviour narrow his fierce eyes even more.

'Are you going to answer me?' he demanded harshly.

Miranda sat forward and then winced as the pain shot straight from her ankle to the remainder of her body. 'My foot!'

The man's eyes travelled from her face to her foot and for a second she thought that he might ignore her expression of pain, but he didn't. He removed his hands from his pockets and bent over to slowly ease her foot out of her ski boot; then he muttered something that sounded very much like an expletive as he saw her swelling ankle.

'What happened?' His long fingers were pressing against various parts of her burning, painful skin. They were cool and skilful and, combined with the relief of not being skewered by those dangerously blue eyes, she sank back against the arm of the sofa and stared upwards at the lofty ceiling.

'I was skiing and I fell,' Miranda said in a small voice and he muttered another impatient oath under his breath. 'I'm sorry,' she felt compelled to add defensively.

'Keep still. I'll be back in a moment.'

She watched his departing back and only felt herself relax when he was no longer in sight.

Trust her to stumble helplessly into a man, the first ever, who intimidated her. He was too tall, too powerfully built, too raw and far too grim. She wondered whether he had disappeared to find something to help her or whether he had simply gone in search of a map so that he could point her in the direction of the nearest other place of occupation and thereby save himself the inconvenience of having her around.

'I don't think it's broken,' he said, emerging with a box in his hand. 'Badly sprained but not broken. How long have you been travelling on it?'

'About half an hour.' Miranda frowned. 'I think. Look, you don't have to do this,' she said as he opened the box and began unravelling a strip of bandage. 'I'm capable of seeing to my own ankle.'

'You mean like you're capable of skiing without injuring yourself? You bloody beginners should stick to the nursery slopes instead of thinking you can ski off-piste because it's more exciting.' He ripped the bandage with his teeth and began stretching it around her ankle, working very slowly and expertly.

'I am not a beginner,' she said coldly. 'I happen to be an extremely good skier.'

The man briefly looked at her with cool disbelief before returning to his task, and Miranda clamped her teeth together firmly. He might have the manners of a warthog but she would not sink to his level. For a start, whether she liked it or not, she was now dependent on him, at least until she could make a phone call and get someone to come and fetch her. She was also too well-mannered to breeze past the normal rules of common courtesy the way he obviously had no qualms about doing.

'How do you know it's not broken?' she asked and he glanced at her again.

'Because I just do,' he said curtly.

'You're a doctor, then, I take it?'

'No, I'm not.'

'Then, who and what are you?'

He didn't answer. Instead he finished with her ankle while she continued to simmer with growing irritation at his attitude. And when he had finished he stood up and strolled towards the chair closest to the fire.

'Are you going to answer me?' She pulled off the woollen hat and her long blonde hair spilled over the arm of the sofa like a sheet of cream silk.

'Let's get one thing straight. You're in *my* house and *I'll* ask the questions. Got it?'

Miranda stared at him open-mouthed.

'When I'm finished asking the questions and I'm satisfied with the answers, you can go and have a bath and get into some of *my* clothes.'

His arrogance hit her like a sledgehammer and left her speechless.

'First of all, tell me just how you happened to be skiing here. Have you any idea how dangerous the vertical slopes to this place are?'

'I—I got caught in an avalanche…'

'Where?'

'Where…what?'

'Where was this avalanche?'

'Near our Val d'Isère resort, as it happens. I…had a bit of an argument with my boyfriend…and…I went skiing to take my mind off things which was when the avalanche happened. Not a very big one but big enough to throw me off course…'

'Bloody irresponsible woman,' he muttered scathingly.

Miranda ignored the interruption. If she had been in possession of her limbs, she would have stormed out of his damned cabin even if the alternative had meant a night on a slope. Unfortunately the option was not available and she bit back her anger.

'Before I could get my bearings, I found myself stuck in a blizzard and, after a while, I didn't have a clue where I was. I—I saw a clump of trees and decided that I'd be better off there if the worse happened and I had to spend the night outside. I was so desperate to get there that I didn't see where I was going and I fell over a protruding stump of tree and sprained my ankle. I then saw the light from your cabin and hobbled over.'

'So no one knows where you are.'

Miranda didn't like the sound of that. She propped herself up on her elbows and looked at him nervously. It occurred to her suddenly that he could be *anyone*. It was a little technicality that had been overlooked in her relief at being rescued from the driving snow and the prospect of hypothermia.

And he was not someone she could fight off should she need to. She was tall, standing a good five feet ten in stockinged feet, but she would put him at least three or four inches taller than her and there was a muscled strength to him that would add power to his height.

She had a sinking feeling when she met his blue eyes that he could read every wayward thought flitting through her brain.

'So...' Miranda cleared her throat '...have I answered all your questions *satisfactorily*?'

'Oh, I haven't asked the most important one yet...' He smiled slowly and linked his fingers on his lap, stretching out his long legs in front of him.

'And what's that?'

'Your name...'

Miranda gritted her teeth in frustration. He had obviously seen the apprehension on her face and had decided to have a little fun at her expense, allowing just sufficient hint of a threat behind his silences to send her nerves skittering.

'Miranda. Miranda Nash.'

'Nash…' He tilted his dark head to one side and Miranda nodded vigorously.

'That's right. You may have heard of my father. Lord Geoffery Nash.' Her voice implied that whilst it might very well be true that no one knew her whereabouts, then it was also true that, should anything happen to her, there would be serious consequences to be paid.

'*Lord Geoffrey Nash* no less…'

'You've heard of him, then?'

'Is that what I said…?' He gave a low, amused laugh which for some reason annoyed her.

'Is there a phone here I could use?'

'The land lines are all dead.' He shrugged his broad shoulders and continued to look at her, though this time with speculation. 'Thanks to this blizzard. And I don't expect them to be up and running for some time yet. The weather forecasts weren't too good for the next couple of weeks ahead.'

'*Next couple of weeks ahead?*' Where, she wondered, appalled, did that leave her?

'Fortunately, I have a cellphone.' He raised his eyebrows expressively and Miranda scowled at him.

'May I borrow it? Please?' she added when he made no effort to move. 'I want to call my dad to let him know that I'm safe and to tell him to get in touch with Freddie and the rest of my friends who might be worried…'

'Why, of course.' He gave a mock bow which further set her teeth on edge, and produced a fist-sized cellular phone which he handed to her with a flourish.

Miranda rapidly tapped in her father's direct office number and after a few seconds was connected to him, smiling as she listened to his frantic overreaction to her situation, which she played down as much as she possibly could. She and her father were members of the mutual adoration society. He doted on her and she adored him. Which was why she guiltily omitted to mention the cause of her predicament, namely an argument with Freddie, whom her father contemptuously referred to as a foolish fop with more money than brains.

'And who is this man you're staying with at the moment?' he rasped down the end of the telephone and Miranda put her hand over the receiver to ask for a name.

'Hand me the phone.' He walked over to her and extended his hand and after a few seconds of internal debate, she let him have it, resenting the way he spoke in a low voice with his back to her, even having the nerve to head out of the sitting room so that all chance of eavesdropping was squashed.

What could he have to talk to her father about? For so long? She impatiently waited for him to return and, when he did, she snatched the phone off him to say goodbye to her father, then she rested the mobile on the table next to her.

'What were you talking to Dad about?' she asked suspiciously. 'And what's your name? Why couldn't you just tell me?'

'Fond of asking questions, aren't you?' He threw another log on the fire and turned to look at her. 'I thought it wise to reassure your father that you weren't going to come to any harm here. My name, by the way, is Luke Decroix.'

'And how did you manage to reassure him?' Miranda asked tartly. 'Did you tell him what a nice, charming, inoffensive gentleman you are?'

'Oh, I think he gathered that from my voice. I also told

him that you would call him every day just to fill him in on how you were. The fact is, I'm stuck with you at least until this blizzard has eased off a bit...'

'*You're* stuck with *me*?'

'That's right.' He gave her a long, measured look. 'I mean, you arrive in a heap on my doorstep and, face it, there's not much you're going to be able to do for yourself for a few days, is there? Not with that ankle of yours?'

'I don't intend to let you take care of me, so you needn't worry.'

'Oh, is that right...? Well, you won't be able to shovel snow and chop logs, will you?'

'You know I can't.'

'What about cleaning...?'

Miranda looked around her—for the first time since she had arrived at the cabin. Downstairs comprised the sitting room, which was quite big with low bookshelves fronting the open fireplace and several battered chairs in addition to the sofa. Through one open door she could glimpse a kitchen and there were a couple of other rooms at the back as well. Wooden stairs led up to a galleried landing which overlooked the downstairs, and off the landing were several rooms, probably bedrooms.

'You've never so much as lifted a duster, have you?' he asked quietly and she flushed. 'What about cooking? Can you cook?'

'I suppose so.'

'You *suppose* so?'

'I—I've never needed to cook. Ethel looks after Dad and me...' Even to her own ears, her résumé sounded woefully inadequate, and she tossed her hair back and glared at him. 'I guess I could try my hand at doing something in the kitchen. It can't be that difficult...'

'What *do* you do?' Luke asked with mortifying curiosity.

'I—I'm a trained interior designer, if you want to know.' Except, she did precious little of that, she thought with a stab of guilt. Her father had funded her course and had even provided her with her first clients, but her enthusiasm had gradually waned; she realised that she had not done anything to further her career for years now. Socialising had left little time for the more serious business of working and, without the need to earn a living, she had found it easy to be diverted.

'That must keep you busy. Does it?'

'Have I asked you what *you* do?' Miranda retorted hotly feeling defensive at the realisation that, if he knew the truth about her idle lifestyle, he wouldn't be very impressed.

'So it *doesn't* keep you busy, I take it,' he replied calmly.

'I never said that!'

'Oh, but your lack of answer tells me that you don't spend your days earning a crust as an interior designer. Which leads me to conclude that you really do nothing with your life except…what…party? Have fun holidays wherever the in crowd happens to be? I know your type.'

'It's important to enjoy life,' Miranda said for the sake of argument, even though she knew that she was on losing ground.

'You'd better go and get changed.' He stood next to her and then grasped her arm with his fingers, help that she reluctantly accepted. 'You can borrow some of my clothes, even though they're probably not quite up to your standard, and then I'll cook us something to eat.'

'Thank you,' she muttered, out of good manners—though she was looking forward to putting on dry clothes.

Whenever she tried to stand, even slightly, on her hurt foot, she could feel her whole body flinch in discomfort. The bandage had made it feel better, or at least had given her the illusion of thinking that it did, but who cared whether she could hop, skip and jump in the morning? She would still be stuck here in ferocious bad weather with this unbearable man who moved from hostility to contempt with the ease of a magician. Through the little panes of the window she could see the snow whipping around outside and she could hear it as well. The low howl of wind and the soft spitting of the snowdrops. It was a nightmare.

'Don't be too proud to ask for help,' he threw in casually, as she clung to the banister and tried to heave herself up, and Miranda looked at him sourly. Blue eyes, a deeper more piercing shade than her own aquamarine-blue and infinitely more opaque, met hers. His eyebrows were dark, the same raven darkness of his hair. But, close to him like this, she noticed his eyelashes, which were thick and long and unexpectedly attractive.

'If you wouldn't mind...' she said, looking away, and he obligingly swept her off her feet and carried her upstairs as though she weighed less than a feather. A huge wave of exhaustion swept over her and she had to fight to keep her eyes open.

It felt so comfortable being carried like this. She could feel the strength of his body against her, like steel. The hands supporting her were large and powerful, like the rest of him; and, unlike most of the men she socialised with, he smelt not of expensive aftershave but of something more masculine and tangy. Very rough and ready, she thought. He would be if he lived here and spent his life chopping logs and skiing.

'There's just the one bathroom,' he said, pushing open

the door with his foot and then settling her on the chair by the bath. 'So make sure you leave it just as you found it. I don't intend to have to clean up after you.'

Without bothering to give her a second glance, he began running the bath, testing the water with his hand, squatting by the side of the bath so that his shirt lifted slightly to reveal a slither of hard brown skin.

'I'd better get you undressed.' He turned towards her and she was propelled out of her lazy observation of him.

'No, thank you!'

'You mean you can do it all yourself? With that ankle of yours?'

'I'm very grateful to have been rescued by you,' Miranda said stiffly, 'but if you lay a finger on me, I swear I'll scream this place down.'

'Oh, will you?' He leaned over her, caging her in with his hands and making sure that there was no place for her to look but at his face. His features were blunt and over-poweringly masculine and she cringed back into the chair like a startled victim of a bird of prey. 'And who do you think will hear you? But...' as quickly as he had leaned over her, he stood back, straightening to his massive height, and looked at her with an insolent lack of respect '...far be it from me to invade your maidenly privacy. Just make sure you clean up after yourself. I don't want to find any of this...' without warning he lifted some strands of her hair between his fingers so that the long fine white-blonde hair trailed over his wrists '...clogging up my plug hole.'

It took one full hour for her to complete her bath. Struggling out of her layers of ski gear was a feat along the lines of running five marathons in a row. And then, when she finally decided that her body would shrivel from over-exposure to bath water, she got out and was confronted with the further indignity of yelling for him from the top of the stairs with a towel wrapped around her and her hair hanging limply wet down her back.

'I wonder if I might borrow those clothes you mentioned?' she told him when he finally surfaced at the bottom of the stairs with a saucepan in his hand.

'I'm sorry?'

'I asked whether I might borrow those clothes you mentioned?' Miranda repeated tersely. The towel barely covered her body. He must have known how awkward she felt standing here like this but either he didn't give a damn or else he frankly enjoyed her discomfort. Or both.

'I heard that bit. I'm waiting for you to finish your request.'

'*Please.*'

'That's much better.' He deposited the pan on the small wooden table at the bottom of the stairs and then headed up towards her. 'You can use the spare bedroom,' he said, pushing open a door to reveal a small, cosy room with its own open fireplace. There was just enough space for the single bed, a dressing table with a mirror and a chest of drawers. Miranda propped herself up against the door frame and looked around it. She was used to sleeping in a double bed. Even when she stayed in hotels, she always insisted on a double bed, however much extra the room might cost. She liked having a lot of space when she went to sleep. Single beds reminded her of hospitals and hospitals reminded her of her mother who had died in one when she had been barely knee-high to a grasshopper.

'Not good enough for m'lady?' For a big man, he moved with disconcerting stealth, she thought, swinging around to face him and finding a bundle of clothes shoved into her hands.

'It's fine. Thank you.'

'Good. Because the only king-sized bed is in my room and my excessive hospitality does have its limits. Now, shall I help m'lady inside?' Without giving her time to answer, he placed his hand squarely around her waist, leaving her no option but to clutch the loosening towel with one hand and place the other around his neck.

'Now...' He stood back and looked down at her with his arms folded '...you can get changed, and I'll be up in fifteen minutes with something for you to eat. M'lady.' He gave a mock salute.

'Could you please stop calling me that?'

'M'lady?' His dangerous blue eyes widened with an expression of ridiculously inept innocence. 'But why?'

'Because it's not my name.'

He didn't bother to answer that. Instead he moved across to the dead fireplace. 'Cold in here, isn't it? But then, I wasn't expecting company or else I would have lit this fire and had the room warm and ready. You'd better get dressed. You're trembling. I'll put your clothes to dry in front of the fire downstairs.'

'Thank you.'

'And I'll bring some logs up later and get this fire going.'

'I would appreciate that.' Miranda could feel goose pimples on her arms from the abrupt change in temperature after the warm bathroom. 'You needn't worry, Mr Decroix...'

'Luke, please. Why stand on formality when we'll be living together?' He inclined his head to look at her over his shoulder, and she realised, with a little start, that it wasn't simply his face that was attractive, but the whole package. In a primitive, masculine sort of way. He had the kind of unchiselled, powerful good looks that drew stares, and she immediately looked away just in case he thought that she was staring.

'My father will more than compensate you for any trouble.'

This time, he turned slowly to look at her and an expression of contemptuous amusement gathered itself in the corners of his mouth and glittered in the blue, brooding eyes. 'How reassuring. And you think that I might need the compensation, do you?'

Miranda edged her way inelegantly to the bed and slipped under the covers with her towel still in place and the bundle of clothes still in one hand; then she drew the duvet all the way up to her chin. If he insisted on ignoring her chattering teeth and continuing the conversation, then she might as well be warm.

'It's only fair after putting you to all this trouble. But most people wouldn't say no to a bit of financial help,' she finally said, awkwardly.

His blue eyes narrowed coldly on her face. 'Oh, dear. Would you have reached that conclusion by any chance because of my ragged clothing?'

'I hadn't noticed the state of your clothing,' Miranda plunged on. 'I have no idea about your financial circumstances...I don't know what you do for a living. But, well...' His shuttered look was hardly encouraging but now that she'd started, she felt compelled to reach some sort of conclusion to her speculations. '...there can't be that many well-paid jobs that you could do from this remote location...can there...?' Her voice trailed off into silence while Luke continued to observe her with embarrassing intensity.

He shook his head with a low laugh, 'I don't live here all the time, *Miranda*.' He paused for a moment, looking as if he was pondering something very deeply. 'In fact,

I'm just looking after this place actually—for the time being.'

'Oh, I see!' That would explain a lot. His English accent, for a start. He was probably one of these nomadic types who made their way round the world doing manual chores for people. Earning a crust.

He didn't say anything. After a few minutes his expression lightened and he shrugged. 'I'll bring you up something to eat. Your foot will feel much better in the morning.'

He didn't call her m'lady again, although he more than made up for the thoughtful omission by bowing grandly at the door before he left; but Miranda no longer had the energy to feel annoyed. She was too sleepy. She would just close her eyes for a few minutes before she changed and he returned with her food.

CHAPTER TWO

THE room was warm. That was the first thing Miranda noticed when she next surfaced. A warm room and she was changed. Her eyes flickered open and for a few seconds she experienced the disorientation that sometimes attacks when the surroundings are new and unfamiliar. Then her memory returned with a crash and the image of Luke's dark, striking and unpleasantly cynical face filled her head.

It was as though the thought had been enough to summon him, because just at that moment her bedroom door was pushed open and she saw the object of her wandering mind filling out the doorway, with a tray in his hands. Sleep had not managed to diminish his suffocating masculinity. In fact, she literally drew her breath in as he dwarfed the small room, primitively forceful despite the tea towel slung over his shoulder.

'So you're up at last.' He moved across to the curtains and yanked them open, exposing a watery grey light and the sight of fast-falling snow. 'Breakfast.' He deposited the tray on the bed and Miranda struggled up into a sitting position.

'How long was I asleep?' She stretched and the sleeves of the oversized grey tee shirt rode down to expose her slender, pale forearms.

'Over ten hours.'

'Over ten hours!'

'I dutifully came with your supper only to find you sound asleep and snoring...'

'I do not snore!'

'How do you know that?' he asked snidely, pulling up a chair so that he could sit and watch her. 'It's not the sort of thing a lover might bring to your attention. Anyway, I lit the fire to get the icicles off the ceiling and left you.' He linked his fingers together and looked as she bit into the toast and then hungrily began demolishing what was on the plate: A fried egg, bacon, baked beans, just the sort of breakfast she had always avoided.

'After I'd changed you, of course.'

Miranda paused with the last bit of toast *en route* to her mouth and started at him. '*You* change me?'

'Shocking, isn't it?' He clasped his hands behind his head and stretched out his legs, crossing them at the ankles. 'Do you think that Daddy might refuse me my much needed financial compensation if he knew?'

'You're not funny!' She had somehow assumed that she had changed herself, even though she had no recollection of doing any such thing, but she could tell from the gleam in his eyes that the man wasn't lying. He had unwrapped the towel from her and had pulled on a tee shirt, and somewhere along the line those big hands of his had touched her shoulders, her stomach, her breasts. 'You had no right!'

'I do beg Your Highness's pardon, but going to sleep with a wet towel around you in a damp room would just have compounded the sprained ankle with a healthy dose of pneumonia.'

'You still had no right! You should have awakened me!'

'I'll try and remember the next time, if you try and remember to stick to the nursery slopes so that there won't *be* a next time. You haven't eaten all your egg up.'

'I've lost my appetite.' She closed her knife and fork and reclined back on the pillow.

'In which case, you'd better try and find it. You're building your strength up and step one is eating all that breakfast, meticulously prepared by my own fair hands.' He leaned forward. 'Maybe you'd like me to feed the rest to you...'

Miranda gave a little yelp of denial and hurriedly ate what was left on her plate, then she wiped her mouth with the paper napkin and folded her arms.

'Now,' he said implacably, standing up to remove the tray and then whipping the duvet off her so that she yelped even louder, this time in enraged discomfort, 'the next thing I advise you to do is test that foot of yours.'

'And would you like to hear what *I* advise *you* to do?'

'Not really. Here, hold my hand and stand up.'

'Or else what...?'

'You don't want to find out,' he said silkily. 'Now, stand up and try that foot of yours.'

When she remained on the bed, he leaned over her and said in a low, razor-sharp voice, 'Shall I just remind you that you're an unwanted and unwelcome intrusion into my house...'

'*Your* house?'

'While I'm looking after it, it's my house. And if you think you're going to play the grand princess and laze around for the next few days, or weeks if this weather doesn't sort itself out, then you're in for a shock. I'm not a man who puts up with the wiles and tantrums of a spoiled little rich girl!'

'How *dare you* speak to me like that?' Her imperious voice, which reflected more than anything else her be-musement at finding herself in the situation she was in and dealing with the man in front of her, failed to strike a chord. Or rather it did. Luke burst out laughing.

'Oh, dear,' he said, sobering up but not sufficiently to stop the occasional cynical chuckle from slipping through. 'Oh, dear, dear, dear. And you wonder why I call you *m'lady*? Now, up!'

Miranda reluctantly swung her legs over the side of the bed, noting with relief that the tee shirt modestly reached down to just above her knees, and grasped his proffered hand.

'Try and put a little weight on it.'

'I can't.'

'Just try, and stop acting like a baby.'

Which did it. She tentatively touched the ground with her foot and discovered as she applied a bit more pressure that the immediate searing pain she had felt the previous day had become more of a persistent, dull discomfort.

'I'll remove the bandage before you get dressed and soak your foot in some cold water and then I'll truss you up again.'

'There's no need. I can do that myself.'

'Should I allow you to do that, I would live for ever in fear of Daddy's avenging wrath.'

Miranda stopped her halting walk and stared up at him. 'I hate that. Why are you so…horrible and *scathing* about me? You don't even know who I am or what sort of person I am! Yet you feel it's all right to make nasty, derogatory comments about me and my father. Daddy always said that the worst snobs are the inverted snobs. He always said that they're the worst because they never give you a chance to prove yourself one way or another. They just assume that because someone has money, then they can't be worthwhile.' She found herself breathing shallowly as she stared up into his blue eyes.

'Is that what you think I am?' he finally asked curiously. 'An inverted snob?'

'Why else would you be so awful? Just because you don't have any money doesn't make it my fault!'

'No, I guess you're right,' he said in an odd voice, 'it doesn't, does it?'

Instead of feeling pleased at this unexpected victory, Miranda felt suddenly nervous. Nervous because she had become quickly accustomed to his hostility and the lack of it was confusing.

'My foot feels a lot better,' she said, to change the subject, supporting herself on his arm as they headed slowly towards the bathroom, where a further unwanted reminder of his ministrations confronted her in the shape of the blue bath towel she had used the night before, neatly hanging over the towel rail.

She sat on the closed toilet seat and watched as he filled a plastic basin with cold water.

'It's freezing,' she gasped as he soaked her foot.

He said, without looking up, 'It'll reduce most of the rest of the swelling. Don't worry. You'll get used to the temperature. There.' He held up her foot and examined it like a butcher sizing up a joint of meat. 'Not very pretty, but it'll do.' Then he carefully rebandaged it, taking his time. 'Now, there's a change of clothes behind you on the ledge and you might want to do something with that hair of yours. Tie it up, perhaps. Not very practical having that mane swinging around, I shouldn't think.'

'Actually,' Miranda informed him coolly, 'a woman's *mane* is her crowning glory.'

'Oh, is that so? And I always thought of her crowning glory was her mind. How much I'm learning from you.' He shot her a brief, patronising grin and then left.

Miranda gingerly stood up and for the first time took a

long look at her reflection in the mirror. Her waist-length blonde hair had been damp when she had fallen asleep, but even so it had dried and now fell in its usual silky curtain around her face. Her wide blue eyes absorbed the stunning prettiness of her features then, as she stripped off the oversized tee shirt, idly scanned the exquisite, slender proportions of her body. These looks, she thought dispassionately, had turned heads and had opened countless doors to the world of beautiful people in which she moved. If she had been dowdy and unattractive, would she have been as popular? Would men have beaten a path to her door, however much money her father had? Probably not. For the first time, she realised that her looks carried a downside. The had attracted men like Freddie, but looks were disposable. None of the men in her brittle world ever seemed to take time out to search for what lay beneath the sparkling veneer.

She very quickly washed her face and changed into yet another tee shirt and a pair of jogging bottoms that had to be tied with the tan leather belt thoughtfully left along with the bundle of clothes. Then she made her way down the stairs, refusing to yell for assistance.

Luke was in the kitchen clearing up and, for a few minutes, Miranda hovered uncertainly by the door, wondering what to do next.

'Make yourself at home,' he said drily. 'I don't bite.'

She edged to the pine kitchen table and sat down.

'How long does this caretaker job last?' she asked, for the sake of asking something, and he turned to look at her with a momentary expression of bewilderment. Then his face cleared.

'Oh, *this* caretaker job?' he said carelessly. 'Oh, not very long.'

'And then you...'

'Move on.'

'Move on to what?' He made a good caretaker, she thought. The kitchen was tidy, with a stack of logs neatly chopped and piled in the corner.

'Other things,' he said vaguely. 'Now, normally I tend to spend the days outside, but this blizzard has put paid to that, so we might as well work out some kind of routine here so that you don't get in my way.'

Miranda immediately began to bristle. 'I won't *get in your way*. I'm more than happy to spend my time reading.'

'Good.' He paused to sit down, spinning the chair back so that he sat on it with his hands loosely hanging over the back. 'Because I have some business to attend to on my laptop and I don't want to feel that you're lurking around waiting to be entertained.'

'I don't expect to be entertained.'

'Don't you?'

'I'm quite happy in my own company.' Miranda paused to digest this and realised that she was very seldom in her own company. Even at night, when she flopped into bed, sometimes in the early hours of the morning, she was always too tried to really spend any time on her own. 'What work do you have to do?' she asked curiously. 'On a computer? I wouldn't have thought...'

'That I was clever enough to use a computer? Or maybe you thought that I'd never even heard of one?' He grinned wickedly at her blushing discomfort. 'News of technological breakthroughs do sometimes drift even to we yokels, you know. In fact, I'll take a small bet with you that *you're* the one who doesn't have a clue how to operate a computer.'

Miranda's face went a shade deeper in colour.

'Mmm,' Luke said pensively. 'Not much point having

a computer on the ski slopes, is there? Or at the races? Or in Mustique for a few weeks over summer?'

'I—I—'

'You—you—what?'

'I learned everything about computers when I was doing my design course,' she said, holding her chin up to counteract the level of defensiveness in her voice.

'Oh, yes, that interior design course of yours.' He was virtually smirking, and Miranda glowered impotently at him. 'Well, wait right here.' He stood up and she watched suspiciously while he disappeared out of the kitchen, only to return minutes later with a sleek black laptop in his hand.

'There, now.' He flicked it open, pressed a few buttons and the screen unfolded into life. 'Why don't you amuse yourself with this for a little while just while I fetch some more logs from the outside shed and do a bit of chopping.' He moved swiftly around the table so that he was bending over her, one hand resting on the table top, the other pressing various icons until an architectural drawing of a house appeared on the screen.

'What's this?'

'This, my dear interior designer, is a house.'

'Whose house?'

'Oh, just a little dwelling my boss has in mind to renovate. He knows I like playing on the computer now and again, so he lent me this file to have a look at.'

Miranda looked at him narrowly. 'Now, why would your boss do something like that?'

Luke's answer was so swift that she almost wondered whether it had been prepared. 'We go back a ways. If you move this little gadget here, called a mouse, hey presto, you can zoom all over the place.'

Miranda gritted her teeth and allowed him to have his

fun. He would be laughing on the other side of his arrogant, handsome face when she presented him with her ideas, even if the whole lot was erased never to be seen again. The last job she had done of any magnitude had been years previously, but she could feel a stirring of interest in her veins as she glanced at the outlines of a house in front of her.

'You mean you babysit his cabin every year?'

'Oh, yes. It's a long-standing arrangement.' He hadn't straightened, so when he spoke his breath brushed against her cheek and into her ear. 'He must have thought that I might get lonesome, stuck out here as I am, hence this little file for me to play with. Little did he know that I would have unexpected company.' He stood up and flexed his muscles. 'You can mess around however you like. Design whatever you want. It can all be deleted. Why don't you go into the sitting room and relax in front of that roaring fire and show me what you can do with this little toy.'

'I guess you do get lonely here for weeks, maybe months, on end,' Miranda said, half to herself, as she settled onto the big sofa, with the computer on her lap. 'How on earth do you fill your time?'

'Loneliness is a state of mind,' he said over his shoulder, as he slung on his waterproof jacket and then pulled on some very thick wool socks and a pair of snow boots that were by the door. 'And it can only be filled when you're at peace with yourself.'

'Well, if you want to spout philosophy, then I'll just get on with a bit of this interior design, shall I?' She felt herself smile and when she looked up at him it was to find the smile returned. It gave her the oddest feeling.

'When I get back from my healthy outdoor fun, you can phone your father. Although...' he opened the door and swirls of snow blew in '…I did call him half an hour ago. On your behalf.'

Miranda looked up, stunned by this piece of effrontery but, before she could demand an explanation, he had left the cabin, slamming the front door behind him.

Her poor dad probably assumed that the man was a genial, middle-aged caretaker with a family tucked away further down the slopes. He would have a fit if he knew what Luke Decroix was like, she fretted. Ten fits, in fact. He would round up the forces and gear up for a rescue mission, not that that would be possible, given the state of the weather. The windows in the cabin were small, but not so small that she couldn't get a glimpse of the leaden skies, barely visible through the continuing blizzard. Lord alone knew where she was. The skiing resort, her friends, the faithless Freddie and all the bijou little cafés seemed like a dream.

She began experimenting on the computer and the wheels of her rusty memory slowly cranked into life as she played around with ideas. Every so often, she looked up and was treated occasionally to the sight of Luke outside, tramping through the snow with a shovel over his shoulder, making sure that the doorway was kept as clear of snow as possible. He was certainly dedicated to his job, if nothing else.

When he finally came back in, he was carrying a basket of neatly chopped logs slung over his shoulder which he dumped on the ground. He didn't say anything, just looked at her. Then he divested himself of his wet waterproofs and his boots and socks. His black hair was slick from the snow and he went to squat in front of the fire, rubbing his hands together and raking them through his hair.

'So you haven't got bored yet with fooling around on

the computer?' he asked, with his back to her. He pulled his thick jumper over his head and stood up, pulling down the shirt underneath. Another tee shirt, this time with some faded design on the front of what was once a bulldog next to a glass of beer. 'What have you done?' He sat down next to her, depressing the sofa so much that she had a job not to slide straight into him, thigh against thigh.

'Not much. Is the snow just as heavy outside?'

'What do you think of the house? Like it?'

Miranda angled the screen away from him, suddenly shy at exposing her efforts to him. 'You promised I could use your mobile to call Dad. Which reminds me...' yes, a good healthy dose of irritation to bring her back on course '...whoever said you could call my father? And how did you get his number? And what did you have to say to him, anyway?'

'Questions, questions, questions. Didn't your mother ever tell you that when a man returns from some hard labour, the last thing he needs is a whinging woman?'

'My mother died when I was eight.'

'Oh, yes. I'm sorry.' He leaned back on the sofa, hooking one foot around the leg of the table in front and pulling it towards him so that he could rest both his feet on the surface. He had replaced his boots with the same worn, tasselled loafers that had greeted her when she had arrived the previous day. He rubbed his eyes, then folded his arms behind his head and looked at her.

His blue eyes were hypnotic. When she looked into them, she had the strangest sensation of giddiness and a feeling that, if she wasn't careful, she could easily fall into their fathomless depths and drown.

'You haven't answered my questions,' she reminded him tartly.

'Oh, so I haven't. Well, if you really want to know, I

have a little method of obtaining the number of the last
call on my phone, which I did last night after you had
called him in his office. And I thought I might as well
touch base, let him know that nothing untoward had happened to his baby during the night. Here, call him yourself
now if you like.' He felt in his pocket and retrieved the
palm-sized phone which he handed to her. Except, he
didn't quite hand it over, more dangled it in front of her
so that she had to reach for it.

Depressingly, her father seemed to have been reassured
by Luke's phone call.

'Might do you a spot of good being stuck in the middle
of nowhere for a few days,' he joked, impervious to her
horror at any such suggestion. Miranda clamped the phone
tighter against her right ear and inclined her body slightly
away from Luke's undisguised interest in what she was
saying and what was being said to her.

'How can you say that, Dad?' she muttered, but the
question was bypassed in her father's sudden need to get
going to a meeting. His driver, apparently, was waiting.
He had to dash but he would be in touch, probably later
in the evening when he was back home.

'I hope he's not too worried about you,' Luke said pi-
ously, reaching out for the mobile and resting it on the
table next to his feet. 'I *did* try and set his mind at rest.
Told him how well you were being looked after. I even
said that I had lent you my laptop so that you could amuse
yourself on it for a couple of hours.'

'I'm sure my father doesn't want lengthy explanations
from *you* on how I'm doing,' Miranda informed him
haughtily.

'So, what have you managed to do? Anything at all?'

'You never bothered to tell me what your boss meant

by *renovating*. Does he intend to knock walls down? What specifications is he after?'

'My, my. I take it you're wearing your technical interior designer hat now?'

'If you want to sit there and smirk, then why don't we just forget this?' Miranda said. 'You can have your little toy back to do whatever it is you need to do and I can't imagine what, and I'll just content myself with one of those detective novels on the bookshelf.'

Luke pulled the computer towards him so that it was partially resting on his lap and looked at what she had done. 'So, you *are* capable of using a computer. Accept my humble apologies for implying otherwise...' When she looked at him, his face was patently lacking in remorse. He was flicking through the rooms she had designed, seemingly interested. 'There's no need for a dining room that big,' he murmured.

'How do you know? Don't tell me: you're so close to this boss of yours that you have insider knowledge into how often he plans to entertain and for how many people. Are you sure this boss is a man and not a woman?'

'Oh,' Luke murmured softly, scrolling through her work and using various icons to magnify certain aspects, 'I'm most emphatically certain on that point.'

'Well, what *does* this man want to do with the house?'

'I gather he intends to move out of London and use it as a base for his work. So, and I'm presuming here, I expect he would want a fairly large working area.'

'What does this man do?'

'Something to do with finance, I believe.'

'You mean he hasn't bothered to bore you with the details?' It was Miranda's turn to smirk and she did so with relish. 'Perhaps he thought that you weren't up to understanding the technicalities of his job.'

'What's this?'

'It's an archway. I've bashed through those two rooms and linked them with an archway. On either side you can incorporate stained-glass windows as features to break the monotony of the brick wall.'

'Very creative. He'll like that touch, I'm sure. And what's this?'

'I haven't finished with that bit yet.'

'That's not what I asked.'

'Well, that bit, if you can picture it…'

'Which might be difficult due to the dullness of my brain…' he murmured, without looking at her, apparently absorbed by her little efforts at the task he had set her with his tongue in his cheek.

'Is a wrought-iron gate—and he should be able to get an original one—separating the bathroom from the bedroom, so there's a feeling of tremendous space.' She could feel two patches of excited colour on her cheeks and remembered that her efforts would be deleted before her enforced stay was over.

'Very imaginative.' He closed the screen, shut the lid of the computer and stood up, leaving a void of coldness next to her. He lazily tipped a couple of logs into the fire, so that it sparked up again, hissing, then he glanced over to the bookshelf and selected a book, tossing it lightly to her.

'What's this for?'

'Reading fodder.'

'And what about my design work?'

'What about it?' he asked, perching on the edge of the low bookshelf and inspecting her face coolly.

'Don't you want me to continue?'

'Sure, if you want. Just thought you might want a

break, though, after all the hard work.' He gave her a slow, challenging smile.

'Meaning...what?'

Luke shrugged his massive shoulders casually. 'Meaning that you might need to take a little time out, get accustomed to doing something other than thinking about what your next temporary pleasure might be.'

Miranda looked at him with a sudden flare of anger. He didn't give up, did he? Now that he had grown used to the thought that she might be around for a few days, interrupting his lifestyle, whatever that might be, he had decided to enjoy himself at her expense. The worst of it was that it hurt. His opinions of her shouldn't matter but for some reason they did. Probably, she thought bitterly, because she was forced to sit them out. She couldn't run away because there was nowhere to run to.

'That's not fair,' she muttered.

'Isn't it? I told your father that this wasn't a five-star hotel and that I would make sure that you were all right and delivered back to him safe and sound, but that in the process you would be expected to work for the favour. He seemed delighted. He obviously knows you better than you know yourself.'

'You told my father, *what*? You have *no right* to discuss me with my father!' she found that she was spluttering in outrage. *'Just who do you think you are?'*

Instead of reacting to her tone, he simply raised his eyebrows, and the silence after she had vented her fury stretched between them like a piece of elastic. He went to one of the deep chairs, picked up the computer and opened it, scrupulously ignoring her presence as he quietly examined something on the screen and began typing on the keypad.

'Will you listen to me when I'm trying to talk to you?'

He didn't appear to have even heard her protest. He simply continued what he was doing and, in a burst of anger, Miranda stood up. It only took a few seconds for her to hobble to the power point and yank out the plug to his computer which died into blackness.

This time he *did* notice her.

His blue eyes became slits and she felt a thrill of sudden, nervous terror skitter through her veins like alcohol. Then he was on his feet, grasping her by her arms so tightly that she cried out.

'Don't you *ever, ever* do anything like that again! Do you understand me?' He shook her slightly and her long hair, which she had made no effort to tie back, swung around her face. She felt like a rag doll at the mercy of a raging bull. 'I will *not tolerate* you stamping your feet like a toddler deprived of a treat whenever you fancy no one's paying you any attention!'

'I'm sorry,' Miranda choked out, dismayed at what she had done and embarrassed to be likened to a toddler. 'You're hurting me!'

He released her but didn't step back. He just continued watching her as she rubbed her arms and she knew that he was making an effort to keep his temper in check. When she glanced up, she could see the vein throbbing in his neck.

'I'm really sorry,' she repeated, to break the deathly silence and deflect the alarming power of his blue eyes.

'Sit down.' The stillness of his voice was as threatening as his roar had been a few minutes ago and Miranda shakily sat back down, leaning forward tensely to accept the brunt of his reprimands. She deserved it. Yanking that plug out of its socket had been the action of a thwarted child and there was no point in trying to use any ham line about acting in retaliation because he hadn't done anything to her. He had ignored her and his patent indifference had stung and had provoked her into a show of puerile stupidity.

'This won't do, Miranda, will it?' He too was leaning forward, his elbows resting on his thighs, his expression hard. 'You're not a child and you must stop behaving like one. Like it or not, you're here with me and you're going to act like an adult. That little display of temper will be the last, do you read me loud and clear?'

Miranda nodded miserably. 'I...' Oh, God. She could feel her eyes beginning to brim over and she hated herself for the weakness. She couldn't remember a time when she had cried in front of anyone, except for her father. She had certainly never shed a tear over any of her boyfriends nor had she ever felt provoked enough by any of them to cry either in their presence or out of it. Not even when she had caught Freddie *in flagrante delicto*. Her pride had been wounded, yes, but her reaction had been one of fury rather than sorrow. Maybe she was going stir crazy because of the isolation.

He waited for her to continue while she stared down at her slender fingers and tried not to gulp too loudly.

'I...enjoyed doing that design work on the computer,' was all she could think of saying. Her mind had become cloudy and she licked her lips and tried to regain control of her thoughts. She sneaked a glance at him and saw that he was still looking at her at least, his head tilted to one side as though making sure that nothing went unheard. 'It's easy for you,' she said defiantly, but her defiance was stillborn.

'Why is it easy for me?'

'Because…you seem happy with your life, moving from place to place.'

For no reason, he looked momentarily uncomfortable with what she had said, but the shadow of unease was soon gone. 'I get the feeling that your father is worried about you.'

Miranda shrugged, too tired to care whether he mentioned her father or not. What did it matter anyway? She wasn't going to be here for ever. She could unburden herself on this passing stranger if she wanted, safe in the knowledge that nothing would come back to haunt her. Briefly, they were sharing the same space, but not for long.

'What does…' he imitated her shrug '…*that* mean?'

'All fathers worry about their daughters,' Miranda said uncomfortably. 'Especially when there's no one else to share the worry with.'

'And what exactly do you give him to worry about?'

'I don't suppose he's too impressed with my lifestyle,' Miranda admitted. Just saying it aloud made her mouth taste sour. It was an admission she had never made to anyone in her life before. 'He thinks that I should settle down…'

'You mean get married?'

'Oh, good heavens, no! I'm only twenty-five!' She laughed at the idea. 'Besides, I can't think of any suitable candidates for the role. If I had ever considered settling down with any of the boys I went out with, my father would have had a heart attack on the spot!'

'Perhaps you should have been looking for a man instead of a boy,' Luke drawled.

Miranda averted her eyes from the blatantly masculine figure sprawling in the chair. 'By *settle down* I mean get a job.'

'Why haven't you? You're talented enough…'

'I'm what…?'

'Talented.' He gave her a slow, amused smile. 'Like me complimenting you, do you?'

Miranda went scarlet. 'I don't care either way,' she informed him nonchalantly. That slow, measured smile made her feel as though she had been physically touched. It gave her goose bumps.

'Good,' he murmured, his eyes still fastened on hers, 'because the last thing I want are any complications.'

CHAPTER THREE

NOR did she.

In fact, she thought, all she wanted to do was clear out of this wretched cabin and get back to London.

At any rate, it was what she firmly told herself. And she was only forced to confront the truth when, after three days of ferocious blizzard, Luke returned from his daily log-chopping exercise and announced that the sky was beginning to look a little healthier.

'What does that mean?' Miranda looked up from the computer and frowned.

'It means, Your Highness, that our friendly blizzard might be going away.' He sauntered over to the fire and removed his jumper. This time, he removed his tee shirt as well, which was soaked. He had his back to her, and Miranda watched, mesmerised, at the movement of muscle beneath skin as he bent slightly to warm his hands.

'Don't call me that,' she said automatically, while her mind struggled to function.

'Sorry.' He half turned to her and grinned with wicked amusement.

'You were telling me about the blizzard,' she said hurriedly, relieved when he turned back to the fire.

'Oh, yes. I think it's clearing.' He was wearing, for the first time, a pair of faded jeans and he began to fumble with the button.

'What,' she squeaked, 'are you doing?'

'Getting out of these clothes. Bloody tripped with the logs in my arms and fell flat on my face in the snow.'

'Good thing you didn't sprain that ankle of yours,' she said, except the thread of tension in her voice didn't quite turn her remark into the light-hearted quip she had hoped. How could she sound light-hearted when she was finding it difficult to breathe? It wasn't physically possible.

'I won't embarrass you, will I?' he asked, pausing to turn completely around and look at her.

His hand was hovering by the top button of his trousers, which had been undone so that the waistband of his jeans curled open, resting lightly on his lean lips and providing a tantalising glimpse of the flat, hard planes of his stomach down, slightly past, his navel.

'I'd prefer to strip down here and leave these clothes to dry by the fire instead of dripping my way upstairs, but if it makes you feel uncomfortable...'

'Not at all!' Miranda trilled in a high-pitched voice. She made sure to look directly at his face although her racing pulse was all too aware of the rest of him; tanned, muscled and disturbingly intrusive. 'I'm the uninvited guest, after all! You go ahead and do exactly as you please.' She busied herself with the laptop computer, glaring at the framework of the room she was working on with her face pressed as close to the screen as it could get without the image becoming blurred in the process.

She could hear the rustle of clothes as he shifted out of his jeans and arranged them on the wooden contraption by the side of the fire, which was permanently on view and almost permanently draped with some item of outdoor clothing.

Couldn't he move any faster? she wondered edgily.

She sneaked a quick look at his feet and quickly resumed her glaring inspection of the screen without focusing on it.

'Your ankle seems almost healed,' he said conversationally.

Miranda replied to the screen. 'Yup.'

'Which room are you concentrating on?' he asked drily.

She said, clearing her throat, 'The kitchen, I think.'

'You think?'

'It's the kitchen!' she snapped, furiously concentrating just in case he decided that a closer inspection of what she was doing was warranted. But he didn't. He just laughed softly and headed upstairs. She found her wits again, breathing a long, shuddering sigh of relief when she knew that he was no longer around.

What did he mean that the blizzard was going? Miranda gently set aside the computer, which she was now utterly familiar and used whenever it was available, and walked slowly across to the window and peered out.

The snow was still falling, but he was right. Sky was visible, blue sky at that.

'Unfortunately...' came the familiar voice from behind her, and she swung around to look at him. His jeans had been replaced with a more presentable pair of trousers than he had worn over the previous few days although the tee shirt was still of the weathered barely-visible-motto variety '...the break in the weather doesn't mean that you'll be able to leave immediately. Sorry.' He lifted his shoulders ruefully. 'The only way out of here is still by ski and until your ankle can fully support the weight, you're going to have to stay put.'

'What about helicopter?'

'What about it?'

'My father could send a helicopter for me. In fact, he almost certainly will want to...'

She wasn't ready to leave. Not yet. The realisation hit

her like a ton of bricks and left her confused and ready for an argument.

Luke gave one of those nonchalant shrugs of his that indicated closure on the subject, and she followed him into the kitchen. Walking was still uncomfortable, but she no longer had to support herself everywhere she went. She could just about manage to lumber along ungracefully but fairly efficiently.

'Well?' she pressed on behind him as he put the kettle on to boil. 'What do you think?'

'If you want to mention it to him when you call then by all means do so.'

'I thought you would have been glad to see the back of me,' Miranda continued nastily. 'After all, you've told me often enough that I'm unwelcome.'

Luke turned around and perched on the edge of the counter, tapping the spoon in his hand softly against his chin. 'A helicopter's fine but I don't suppose it's occurred to you that the snow is still falling fairly heavily and vision might be obscured? Or maybe it occurred to you, but your craving to be back in the swing of the fast lane in London conveniently overrode any guilt that you might be endangering other people's lives in the process? Ah, no. I see that possibility hadn't occurred to you at all. Now, why am I not surprised when you're so used to getting what you want?'

'Not with you!' The words were out before she could call them back.

'No, my darling, not with me.' He said the word *darling* with the brush of soft caress in his voice although his eyes were dangerously cool and brooding. 'Now lunch. I think it's time you started investigating what can be done in a kitchen.'

Which made it sound as though she had spent the past

few days in a collapsed, pathetic and useless heap on the sofa playing with the toy, as he liked to describe it. She had obeyed his orders and made sure that the bathroom was always clean and free from the long blonde hair, which he apparently saw as a hindrance; her bedroom was spotless, despite the fact that making up her bed was only now getting easier.

'I thought you enjoyed cooking,' she said sweetly. 'You said you liked to cook because the last thing you needed in your busy, nomadic life was a woman around thinking that she could win you through her food.' It was surprising that they had managed to have any conversations at all, she thought, considering he was fairly beastly to her most of the time, but she now realised that they had spent most of their evenings chatting, in the absence of anything else to do. He had even started teaching her how to play chess, although, typically, he had refused to play below his high standard in order to accommodate the fact that she was a beginner.

'Did I say that?'

'You did,' she said smugly, 'after a bottle of wine.'

'You'll have to get rid of that hair of yours if you're gong to be of any use to me,' he said abruptly. 'Long hair and cooking don't make a happy combination.'

'I'll tell it to go away, shall I?' She shook it away from her face.

'No, I will. Sit down.'

Miranda obligingly sat and watched as he rustled in a drawer and then moved behind her. When she was about to turn her head to follow him, she felt his hands on either side of her face and her body froze in total compliance.

He began to brush her hair. In the small kitchen, with the snow swirling madly outside and only the noise of the clock on the wall to compete for sound, the gesture seemed suggestively erotic. The feel of his hands as the brush stroked her hair away from her face started a drum roll of steady excitement pulsing through her veins and she forced herself to relax, closing her eyes and dipping her head backwards so that he had to gather all her hair in one hand while he brushed with the other.

'Like this, do you, m'lady?' he asked softly, amused as he carried on brushing; Miranda murmured something by way of assent. Her whole body had relaxed now, with her arms falling on either side of the chair like a rag doll's and her legs stretched out in front of her.

'And do you have a little woman who comes in every day to do this?' His deep voice was rich with a hypnotic, teasing familiarity. Miranda didn't open her eyes, although her mouth curved into a smile.

'A little man, actually. Or rather, a great, big, strong hunk. Twice a day he brushes my hair one hundred times.'

'A great, big, strong hunk. Mmm. That's the type you go for, is it?'

Maybe it was because they weren't facing each other and she didn't have to do battle with those penetrating cobalt eyes, but Miranda could feel herself falling in with this light, strangely invigorating, banter. She squirmed like a cat finding a better position and loosely linked her fingers together on her stomach. The jogging pants he had lent her were too long and she had rolled them several times at the waistband. She idly played with the overlap of stretchy material, rolling her thumbs on them, smiling contentedly.

'The hunkier the better.' She giggled. 'Sadly, I have yet to meet anyone fitting that description.'

'You mean Freddie wasn't a great, big, strong hunk?' His voice was lazy and only mildly curious. Just conversationally passing the time of day, it seemed to imply.

'He was tall, at any rate.' Well-built enough, Miranda thought languidly, but soft and well-manicured; baby soft.

'Care to tell me what happened between you two?'

'Oh, the usual. I caught him with his hands on another woman. A curvy, dark-haired Italian who couldn't have been more than eighteen and should have been cleaning our chalet instead of unbuttoning her blouse to my ex-boyfriend.' She gave a snort of derisory laughter. 'I hit the roof, skied off and the rest is history.'

'Were you jealous?'

'I was angry, but, no, I wasn't jealous. I'm not a jealous type of person.'

He began to massage her scalp and Miranda gave a little moan of sheer pleasure. Free of any tangles, her long hair spilled over his rhythmically moving fingers like a waterfall.

'I take it from your tone of voice that you've recovered from your heartbreak?'

There were alarm bells ringing somewhere. In her head, she thought. Because something was telling her that this easy but intensely personal conversation was dangerous somehow.

'My heart was never broken,' she informed him drowsily. 'I was going to break up with Freddie anyway. He was dull, dull, dull. You wouldn't believe the bottles of after-shave he got through! He even had facials once a month.'

'And has m'lady's heart *ever* been broken?' His voice insinuated itself into her head and was as pleasurable as the fingers pressing gently against her scalp.

'Nope. Has yours?'

'When I was thirteen I was forced to face the unpalatable fact that my high school French teacher didn't fancy me.'

'And that's the closest you've come to having your heart broken?' Miranda teased.

'Shocking, isn't it? By the ripe old age of thirty-four, I should have had my heart broken at least three or four times.'

'Maybe your wandering lifestyle doesn't allow women long enough to be around to get to you.'

'Oh, I don't think that's it at all,' he said with a low laugh and she had a sudden, jolting image of Luke with other women and she felt the sour bile of some primitive emotion rip through her. All these women, she thought, who were undaunted by his lifestyle, who were probably prepared to follow him to the ends of the earth because, as she had seen for herself, when he wanted to be charming, he could entice the birds from the trees. Just like he was doing now, lulling her into this little game of confidences, so that she could admit that her love life was a mess and always had been. She pulled herself forward and held her hair in pony-tail.

'Have you got something I could tie this back with, then?'

'Will a rubber band do?'

'Rubber bands are no good for my hair,' Miranda told him irritably, 'but I suppose it'll have to do.' She reached behind her with a free hand and then flicked her hair secure with the rubber band and brought her legs and the rest of herself back to solid ground. She would have to remind herself that solid ground was precisely where she belonged. Reality was waiting for her just around the corner and it wouldn't do to fall victim to any fantasies. Nor to be lulled into imagining that this bizarre relationship, into which she had found herself catapulted, was somehow reality. It wasn't.

'You were going to teach me how to cook? Not that I don't already know.'

'I thought you said that your faithful housekeeper did all those mundane tasks.' He strolled around the table so that he was facing her once more.

'I never said that cooking was a *mundane task*,' Miranda responded tartly. At least they were back to their normal, bouncing-sarcasm-off-each-other routine but, she realised with dismay, that she no longer found his jibes offensive. Somewhere along the line, the tenor of his voice when he referred to her as m'lady or Your Highness had altered. It was no longer laced with the aggressive hostility that had been so apparent when she had first arrived. When, she wondered, had that happened?

And she had stopped being defensive. Her irritation at some of the things he said was a display more of habit than intent.

'Oh, I just assumed…'

'Because,' she rounded on him, 'you spend all your time *assuming* too much!'

'Why the sudden display of vitriol, Miranda? Didn't you enjoy talking to me when I was combing your hair? Or did you think that I was getting a little too close to the real Miranda?'

The man saw far too much! She glowered at him impotently and he smiled with feline, satisfied speculation at her flushed face.

'You're not as shallow as you pretend, are you? You babble along with the best of them but, underneath, something inside is stirring, isn't it? Looking for more? Tut, tut. Dangerous situation.'

'I suppose with all this time on your hands you've got nothing better to do than drone on the minute you find yourself in company!' Miranda shot back, and he grinned, untouched by her wayward dart. 'I detect a severe case of company starvation! Perhaps the owner of this house should give you a dog so that you can bore him to death with your opinions!'

Luke burst out laughing. 'Methinks,' he said when he had sobered up, 'the lady doth protest too much.'

'Methinks,' Miranda replied, 'we'll have no lunch if the so-called chef doesn't stop nosing into my life!'

He was still grinning fifteen minutes later after he had forced his scowling protégé to recite a summary of her culinary abilities.

'Rusty, in other words,' he summarised, when her stuttering résumé had reached a dead end. 'Well, we'd better set that straight if you're going to repay my generous hospitality by looking after me for a change now that your ankle's on the mend.'

'I didn't realise that that was part of the deal.'

'Oh, didn't you? Maybe I didn't make myself clear enough in that case. Look in that cupboard over there and fish out some onions. There's garlic in the fridge. We'll start with something simple, shall we? First of all, fill a saucepan with water and let's put it on to boil. That'll require some ingenuity as you'll have to light the stove and place the saucepan squarely over the fire.'

Miranda was tempted to place the saucepan squarely over his head.

'Now,' he carried on in the overpatient voice of someone addressing a slow learner of dubious intelligence, 'put a pinch of salt in the water. Just a pinch.'

'I know what a pinch of salt is.'

'There, very good. Now onions. Peel and chop roughly.' He slid two onions across to her and Miranda painstakingly removed the brown skin. Really, this was something she hadn't done for quite some time. Not, in fact, since she had experimented in her food and technology class as a kid.

Instead of busying himself by being useful, he adopted a watchful pose by the kitchen counter, perched on the edge, arms folded.

'I'm surprised you're not an expert cook after going to finishing school,' he commented, as she clumsily peeled one layer of onion skin only to be confronted with another layer in need of stripping. 'Didn't they teach you girls all about haute cuisine along with deportment and the importance of knowing how to set a table and identifying which glass to use for which particular alcoholic drink? Useful pointers like that?'

'I didn't *go* to finishing school,' Miranda said coolly. 'Haven't you got anything to do other than stand there and look at me?'

'Nope.'

'I must be more fascinating than I thought, in that case.' She turned to look at him and saw in her mind's eye the image of him with his fingers resting lightly on that top button of his jeans, his torso lean and muscled, and she swallowed convulsively.

'Why didn't you go to finishing school? I thought that was essential on a CV for girls like you.'

'Girls like me?' Miranda paused in her chopping of the onions and turned to look at him squarely in the face, her hand on the knife.

He shrugged. 'Pretty young things with more money than sense.'

Her hand gripped the handle of the knife so hard that it hurt. He made her sound like a Barbie doll and, in all honesty, she could see where his opinions stemmed from, but it stung. She returned to the onions and furiously chopped them.

'My father disapproves of finishing schools,' she muttered grudgingly.

'Wise man.'

'I'll make sure to pass the compliment on. Now, what next?'

'Mushrooms. Canned, I'm afraid. I stock this place to last a certain length of time but, for obvious reasons, fresh food can be a bit dicey if the weather's like this and I can't ski to the nearest shop. Bacon.' He slid a packet across to her and she opened it, her mind still rankling after his high-handed summary of her character. 'Now you need to put the rice to boil. Have you ever boiled rice?'

'Have you ever been pleasant?'

He laughed and pushed himself away from the counter so that he could tip a generous portion of rice into the boiling water, along with a stock cube and some seasoning.

'And since when are you so qualified to launch into speeches about my background?' This time it was her turn to watch him as he took over the cooking, working expertly at frying various ingredients together, letting the lot simmer in a can of tomatoes flavoured with a touch of Tabasco sauce. 'What's your background? The university of life, I imagine?'

He nodded. 'Via Cambridge.'

'*You* went to *Cambridge University*? Ha!'

'Why do you find that so difficult to believe?' He dumped all the dirty dishes into the sink and tossed a sponge so that Miranda could make herself useful by wiping the counters. 'I'm hurt.'

You're hurt? she thought. And I'm the Queen of England!

'What did you study there?'

'Law and economics.'

Miranda burst out laughing. 'You expect me to believe that you went to one of the top universities in England to study law and economics and then ended up dong this to fill in your time?'

'Actually, I expect you'll believe exactly what you want to believe.' He began washing the dishes with the expertise of someone used to doing their own domestic chores; and, after he'd pointedly handed her a dry tea towel, she reluctantly positioned herself alongside him so that she could dry the dishes.

'Why didn't you become a lawyer?' she demanded, not to be deterred by his non-answer of an answer. She couldn't believe that he had any university degree in any such subjects, although there were things that didn't quite add up about him. Nevertheless, she had met so many men in her time who did relatively little with their lives despite their exalted backgrounds that accepting his caretaker story at face value had not been particularly difficult.

'Or an economist? Or whatever it is that people do after they've studied economics?'

'Perhaps the simple life beckoned...' Luke said sanctimoniously. 'Fresh outdoor air in winter, a chance for a poor yokel like me to see the world.'

Miranda looked at him dubiously, wondering why she suspected that he was play-acting when there was no reason for him to do so.

'And in the summer?' she persisted. 'Where do you go?'

'Where do *you* go?' he asked, turning the question on its head and moving away to dry his hands.

'Oh, sometimes to the country,' Miranda said vaguely. 'To enjoy the simple pleasures of rambling and exploring the great British countryside?'

She flushed and tossed her head in a manner that could either have been interpreted as agreement or adamant denial. Fortunately, before he could drag any further revelations out of her, there was the bubbling sound of boiling water spilling over and he forgot his line of enquiry in his salvaging of their lunch. Then the culinary programme resumed, with yet more detailed instructions, which she obeyed with somewhat more alacrity this time considering the other option was to admit to yet more details of her daily life. Her aimless daily life as she was fast beginning to think.

Stuck in this vacuum, she had been forced to confront her life; and what she had seen, even without Luke's heavy handed, patronising observations, had brought a sour taste to her mouth. She couldn't believe that the years had rolled by in a blurry mist of fast-paced, pointless activity, self-indulgence and the company of people whose friendship would probably crumble if ever put to the test.

'At the risk of disturbing your thoughts,' he whispered silkily into her ear and Miranda jumped, 'you still have one or two finishing touches for this meal. Garlic bread in the freezer. Stick it in the oven. I'll open a bottle of wine.'

'At lunch-time?'

'Wildly decadent, I agree, but very complimentary to our little home-cooked risotto.'

Despite the company she had moved in, Miranda had never fallen victim to drink. She enjoyed the occasional glass of wine but anything beyond that made her sleepy and gave her headaches. For the past few evenings, she had sipped at a glass with her dinner, usually tipping the rest down the sink.

'Drink and enjoy,' he cajoled, handing her the glass. 'Who knows? Tomorrow the snow may be back to normal and Daddy can send his helicopter out to rescue you. Then you'll be free to leave this primitive little cabin behind and return to your gilded cage.'

'And not a minute too soon!' she snapped, raising the glass to her lips and swallowing the lot in three hefty gulps. She instantly needed to sit down. And she did, sticking both her feet onto another of the kitchen chairs which she pulled closer to her. 'Anyway,' she continued thoughtfully, 'this cabin isn't primitive. It's small, but it's comfortable. And the furnishings might be old but they're of good quality.'

'You noticed, did you?'

'Of course I did! Have you forgotten that I hold a degree from the university of shopping?' She gave a little snigger at her own expense and accepted another glass of wine from him. 'I can spot quality from a mile off. Handy trait, wouldn't you say?'

'Only in a thief.'

Miranda laughed. 'Now, there's an option I'd never considered. Cat burglar.'

'The hair would give you away. Too blonde. You could never get away with blending into the night.' He drained his glass as he began setting the table for them and she rose to her feet to help him. 'You would have to cut it short and dye it brown.' He ladled two heaping portions of risotto onto plates and handed one to her, then he sat down opposite her.

'That would appeal to you, wouldn't it?' Miranda said, eating voraciously. Her constant weight-watching mechanism of picking at her food had vanished ever since she had stumbled to the cabin.

'What makes you say that?'

'Oh, just the way you disapprove of all this inconvenient hair of mine.' She helped herself to some more wine.

'Now, now. How can you say that when I spent fifteen minutes brushing it?'

There was amused irony in his voice but, when their eyes tangled across the table, she noticed that his expression was unreadable and a little shiver of giddy awareness shot through her. He was all man. Not just in his physical build, but in the way he moved and the manner in which he conducted himself. Rough, raw, sex appeal and, as she finished her second glass of wine, she wondered what it would be like to make love to him, to lie naked in a bed with him and let him turn all his masculine, vital magnetism onto her. What would it be like to be the sole target of those penetrating blue eyes, clouded with passion?

Face it, she thought dizzily as her body responded to the thought, there would be no consequences. He didn't move in her circles, didn't know any of her friends, and she would never see him again once she had left his cabin behind.

The prospect of the snow letting up within the next twenty-four hours, making it possible for her to leave, either by helicopter or on skies to the nearest town, because her ankle was more or less fully recovered, lent her passing speculations an exciting edge of urgency.

'My hairdresser brushes my hair,' Miranda said, her eyes glittering from the heady combination of unaccustomed wine consumption and the tantalising, erotic turn of her thoughts. 'Doesn't mean he likes it or even finds me attractive for that matter.'

A deathly silence greeted this remark as Luke paused to look at her with his food *en route* to his mouth. Even without looking at him, feigning absorption in her food, she was aware of the shift in atmosphere. Suddenly there was a crackling electricity between them. Every pore in her body was aware of it and she wondered whether he was aware of it as well.

'This food's fantastic. How did you learn to cook? Were you taught? A vital culinary course between the law and economics degree?'

'Necessity is the mother of invention, as they say,' Luke murmured. 'Wouldn't you agree?'

'Absolutely.' She sneaked a quick glance at him from under her lashes to find him looking at her. With a quick flick of her wrist she released her hair from its constraining elastic band and shook her head, like a young filly shaking its mane. Then she sat back and sighed.

'I can't eat another mouthful.' Actually, she wasn't lying. She had eaten several mouthfuls too many. 'I have no idea what's happened to my appetite. I've eaten like a horse since I've been here and I don't even have the excuse of good, healthy outdoor exercise to work it all off.' She drained her glass and felt a wild adrenaline rush as she poured herself another. 'I shall return to England horribly fat and be forced to spend six months continuously at the gym just to get back to my former shape.' She twisted in her chair to inspect her supposedly rapidly expanding waistline and was aware that Luke had closed his knife and fork and was inspecting her inspecting herself with a closed expression, his hands nonchalantly behind his head.

'I've an idea!' She could feel the brightness in her cheeks and realised that she had never in her life before felt so *alive*. The world was a wonderful place, laden with possibility. 'Don't you want to hear what it is?' she asked, when he didn't say anything.

'I don't thing you should have any more wine.'

'That's a very boring response to my question,' Miranda told him loftily.

'Perhaps I'm a very boring person.'

They both knew that that was utterly untrue. Arrogant, forbidding, massively self-controlled but also witty, sharp, intelligent. Never boring.

'I think we should go outside,' she said. 'I've been cooped up in this cabin for days now and I need to get a bit of fresh air. Plus the exercise. I need to get a bit of exercise. I haven't been as sedentary as this for years, sitting in one spot, doing nothing. Can't we get all wrapped up and have some fun in the snow? Please?' She would have done her best doe-eyed look but felt that that might put him off rather than spur him on; and spurring him on now seemed to be the one thing in the world she desperately wanted to do.

'It might do you a bit of good,' he murmured, making his mind up and getting to his feet. 'If you think you can actually stand up properly.'

'Oh, my ankle's fine!' Miranda said gaily and he raised his eyebrows in amusement.

'I wasn't actually thinking about your ankle.'

'What were you thinking about?'

'The alcohol level in your blood,' he said drily, holding up the empty bottle of wine, most of which, she realised, she had single-handedly consumed.

The ski clothes she had arrived wearing were folded in

a pile on a chair next to the fire and, without bothering to remove anything, she wrapped the scarf around her neck, stuck on her padded jacket, socks, ski pants, boots and, as an afterthought, her woollen hat, which had not been too clever for blizzard weather on the road to nowhere, but would do for snow outside the cabin.

Then she stood back and looked as he donned his usual waterproof garb.

Tomorrow she would be gone. Or by the latest, the day after. But today…today felt like none other, and she had no intention of letting it go.

CHAPTER FOUR

AFTER the warmth of the cabin, magnified a thousand times by the heat induced by the wine, outside was a shock to the system. Miranda felt her face tingle as the cold slammed against it; then she gradually became acclimatised and tentatively edged her way further outside, like an invalid trying to walk unaided for the first time.

The snow was still falling, but already she could detect its lessening force. She had told her father on the telephone that morning that she would be back home within days but, even when she had said it, home had still seemed a distant place. It didn't seem quite so distant now that she was outside and could see the dramatic clearing of the weather.

Luke had gone ahead of her, towards the small shed, and she followed in his direction, clumping through the drift in her ski boots and only feeling the very faintest of twinges in her ankle as a reminder of her accident.

'How does it feel?' he asked, with his back to her, as he surveyed the pile of uneven logs stacked in the corner.

'Oh, fine. Look.' He turned to look at her and Miranda walked a few paces towards him. 'Would you notice that I'd ever had a sprain?' She had closed the distance between them so that only a few feet separated them.

'No,' he said flatly. 'As good as new.' He returned to his inspection of the log pile and then rummaged around until he had removed a hefty piece of wood, which he placed on a low cutting table against the side of the wall. 'What are you going to do when you get back?' He picked up the axe and with one clean, powerful swoop divided the log neatly into two, then he repeated the process until there was a small bundle of logs which he flung into a basket on the ground.

'Who knows?' Miranda said. For the first time, she wished that he would look at her instead of those damned logs which he seemed intent on chopping. 'Do you think I ought to try and go back to my interior design?'

If the mountain wouldn't come to Mohammed...

She edged sideways, carefully positioning herself more or less in direct line of his eyes.

It was invigorating being outside for the first time in what felt like decades, but even more invigorating was the craving she had brought out into the open. She had aired it, acknowledged it and now it needed to be satiated. Just the thought of that seemed to make her pulses race even faster.

'Why not?' He shrugged, still not looking at her, as though indifferent to whatever future lay ahead of her. 'It might provide more of a challenge than flitting around the globe looking for distractions.'

'It might.' She paused and appeared to give the matter a great deal of thought. 'But then again, thrill-seeking can be quite a challenge in itself.'

Luke glanced across to her but, because the shed was darker than outside, it was impossible to decipher what he was thinking. Not that it was ever easy to see what was going on in that head of his.

'Don't you agree?' she said, pressing him.

'Depends what you want out of life, I suppose,' he said noncommittally. 'But looking for thrill after thrill, as far as I am concerned, is like a drug, and sooner or later the effect wears off, and what then? You still have to confront all those issues you've spent a lifetime avoiding.'

'It's dark in here, isn't it?' Miranda said, diverting what was turning out to be a gloomy subject. She didn't much want to consider any what then? kind of questions. Her head was filling up pretty fast with them already. 'Shall we go outside? Have some fun?'

'What kind of fun did you have in mind, Miranda?' This time he did look at her, and in the cold semi-darkness of the shed, his eyes glittered like a tiger's.

'We could…build a snowman,' she suggested. 'Then, when I'm gone, you can look at it and remember me.' She wondered what she would remember *him* by and realised that she didn't want to *remember* him. She wanted to continue waking up to him, hearing his voice, responding to every nuance of his voice and every glance in her direction.

'Forget it. I'm obviously in your way out here,' she said tightly, and walked out of the shed, back into the glaring light outside.

She hadn't expected him to follow her and was only aware that he had, when he said from behind her, 'All right. Let's build your memory, shall we? A snowman.' He caught up with her so that they were now walking side by side. 'Seems a little inappropriate, wouldn't you agree? Too squat and circular.'

'There's no need to humour me,' Miranda said sulkily. 'I know you find me a bore and shallow.'

'Whoever said that?' He turned to tilt her face up to his, his gloved finger under her chin. 'Did *I* say that?'

'You didn't have to.'

'*Now* who's making the sweeping assumptions?'

She looked at him hesitantly.

'The snow awaits, m'lady.' He gave a large, theatrical bow, still looking at her, and she allowed herself a small smile. 'Of course, we'll have to tone down the curves a bit...'

'How can we build a skinny snowman?'

'Skinny?' He laughed softly and she felt that little tingle of gut-wrenching awareness slither around inside her. 'From what I recall, not all of you is skinny.' He knelt and began to shape some snow into the beginnings of their snow woman and Miranda joined him. Every so often his gloved hand would brush against hers and she didn't pull hers back but pretended not to notice the casual contact.

'I don't think you should feel insulted if there's not much of a striking resemblance when we're finished,' he said, as they completed the base and moved onto stage two.

'I'll try my best,' Miranda promised. Even building a stupid snowman, there was an air of concentration about him that sent a little shiver up her spine. Would he be like that in bed? Concentrating on *her*? 'And will you think of me when you look at it?' she asked lightly and he flicked her a glance. This time, feeling very bold, she held his gaze until he was the first to look away.

'Why do you think I'll need a snowman to remind me of you? In actual fact, I have an excellent memory.'

'Which goes hand in hand with your sense of modesty?'

He gave a low, sexy laugh. 'Which both trail behind my burning inclination to curiosity. Which makes me wonder what game you're playing at the moment.'

'Me?' Miranda opened her eyes wide, genuinely surprised at what he had said. 'Playing games?'

'And don't flash those innocent baby blues at me.' He caught her gloved hand in his and brought his face very close to hers. 'For a lady who lives in the fast lane, you're as transparent as a girl of sixteen.'

'And what exactly do you see on my transparent face?' she asked, cheeks burning.

'What any man would see when a woman follows him around with her eyes.' Out here, in the unforgiving winter sunlight, his eyes looked even more scorchingly blue and she could see the fine lines that added character to his face. 'You've been giving me hot little looks ever since we had lunch. Did you think I hadn't noticed?'

'I have not!' But her declaration of protest was tinged with guilt and he picked up on it with a triumphant little laugh.

'Liar.'

For a few fraught seconds they stared at one another and she could feel her heart thudding like an engine in her chest. His mouth was only inches away from his. She very nearly swooned like some maiden in a Victorian novel at the thought of kissing him, of those sensual lips of his touching hers, exploring her trembling mouth.

'And what I want to know is *why*.' He stood up and she remained a while hunched on the snow with a dazed expression on her face. Then she stood up as well.

'I don't know what you're talking about,' Miranda said faintly. Oh, did she know what he was talking about! She wanted him. She wanted him to want her. She just hadn't realised that she had been quite so obvious about it. Despite her highly social life and the fact that she had always had no end of young men queuing up to take her out, actually *wanting* a man and wanting him to notice her, to want her too, was completely an alien sensation. Handling it was like playing a new game, the rules of which were unknown.

'Shall we carry on this interesting little discussion inside?'

'But what about our snowman? It's not finished yet,' she babbled.

'Oh, I think our little snowman can wait a while, don't you? Like I said, curiosity has always been one of my foibles and right now I can't wait to see where this is leading.'

He walked towards the cabin, raking his gloved fingers through his hair to free the snow, not pausing to look back and see whether she was following or not. Because, she thought helplessly, he knew that she would be. He pushed open the cabin door and then stood back to remain holding it open, allowing her to sidle past him and, in an embarrassed flurry, remove her gloves and hat while scrupulously avoiding eye contact.

She unzipped her jacket with her back to him and struggled out of her waterproof ski pants, feeling like a stripper on a stage, even though the outer layer of clothing only revealed the old clothes she had been wearing underneath. She could hear him behind her, doing the same; and she could *feel* him, could feel his hot, curious eyes on her back, sending little chills of goose bumps skittering along her arms.

'So,' he said, when she had finally found the courage to turn around, 'are you going to continue denying everything or are you going to tell me what's going on?'

'I think I'd like another glass of wine.'

'Dutch courage?' He laughed. 'Sit down right there and wait for me.' He returned minutes later with a glass for them both and sat down on the sofa next to her, depressing it with his weight. 'Now look at me and talk to me. Tell me what's on your mind. I can be a very sympathetic listener.' He was looking at her lazily and Miranda gulped a mouthful of wine, hoping to recapture the heady recklessness she had felt two hours before.

'Are you going to miss me, my darling?' he drawled. 'Do you want me to give you a couple of nights to remember so that when you cuddle down in your cold, cold bed in England you can think of me? You can touch yourself and close your eyes and have a few scorching memories to remember me by?'

'That's crude!' Miranda gasped, but his words had sent a thrill of dampness down through her body.

'But I'm a crude man, aren't I? Is that what turns you on? The fact that I'm nothing like those pretty boys you've been accustomed to dating?'

He might as well be touching her for the electric response his silky words were generating inside her. And he knew it. He could see it written in bold letters all over her flushed face, she was sure.

'Is that the little game you're playing?' He leaned forward and took a strand of hair between his fingers, curling it around them with a little smile on his dark face. 'Haven't I paid you enough attention while you've been here and, now that you're more or less ready to go, you want me to notice you?'

'I...' Miranda's mouth felt as though it was stuffed with cotton wool.

'I don't think your father would approve,' he murmured softly, releasing her hair.

'My father's not here!

'Ah.' His mouth curved into a knowing smile. 'He's not, is he?' He drained the remainder of his wine and sat back. 'So tell me what happens next. You know the rules of this game. I don't.'

Miranda took a deep, flustered breath.

'Now, don't be shy,' he instructed. He linked his fingers together and cocked his head to one side in expectation.

'This is ridiculous,' she spluttered, lifting her chin.

'Desire, lust…is never ridiculous,' he told her gravely. 'Would you like me to take charge, Miranda?'

As if he would be doing her a favour! She tried to stimulate some self-righteous anger at that but instead found that the thought of him taking charge was even more of a turn on. He stood up abruptly and went across to the windows, drawing the curtains until the room was plunged into darkness, relieved only by two small table lamps which he switched on before sitting back down, this time on the chair.

'Take your clothes off.'

'W-what?'

'Take your clothes off,' he repeated. 'And don't be timid. After all, I've seen your naked body once already; although it has to be said that a sleeping naked figure is quite substantially different from a wide awake and highly charged one.'

'You want to *watch me get undressed*?' she asked, shocked, and he grinned at her bemusement.

'You make it sound like an unnatural desire. Don't tell me you make love by stripping under the covers so that no man can appreciate your body.'

'Well, no…' But pretty close, her frantic expression was telling him. She had certainly never performed a striptease for anyone in her life before, had never even considered it!

'I always say there's a first time for everything.'

Miranda slowly got to her feet and stood in front of him, feeling exposed and, yes, he was right, highly charged. As she reached to the bottom of the tee shirt to pull it over her head, all sense of vulnerability flew out of her head and she gave a little smile as he sat forward slightly, his nostrils flaring as though to capture her scent from where he was sitting on the chair.

She slowly drew the tee shirt upwards, pausing when she knew that a slither of skin would be visible. She had to remind herself that she had been the one to make the advance, which surely must mean that she was in control. She pulled the soft jersey higher, feeling it slide deliciously across the bare skin of her stomach, her ribcage, then over her bra, which, along with her briefs were the only two items of clothing she was wearing from her original garb.

Miranda loved her underwear. She never thought that a woman should give up when it came to what she wore beneath her clothes. Her bra, accordingly, was black, lacy and plunging. She heard him give a grunt of intense satisfaction as she pulled herself free of the tee shirt and tossed it lightly on the ground next to her.

It didn't matter that he had shown her no interest sexually since her arrival. He was interested now. Very interested. And his reaction to her spurred her on. She felt wild with excitement and incredibly daring.

In fact, she had never felt so excited in front of a man before. His drooping blue eyes as they roved over her body was a powerful aphrodisiac.

She slipped her fingers under the waistband of the oversized jogging bottoms, curling them down until her lacy briefs peeped below her belly button.

A little music, she thought, would have been perfect, although the stillness in the cabin was as erotic as any slow number she could think of.

She eased the jogging bottoms slowly down and stepped out of them, kicking them to one side where they joined the tee shirt. When she reached behind her back to unclasp the fastening to her bra, he stopped her.

'Come closer.'

Miranda walked towards him while his eyes followed her every movement.

'Now.' He sat back and watched as she unfastened the bra and her milky-white breasts spilled out of their restraints, settling against her ribcage.

'You have beautiful breasts,' he murmured. 'Nice, big nipples. Let me see you touch them…'

She felt a dizzy rush of blood to her head and was dimly aware of his sharp intake of breath as she rubbed her nipples with her fingers so that the tips jutted provocatively towards him, as if issuing an invitation to plunder.

He crooked his finger for her to step yet closer. Then, when they were within touching distance of each other, he traced a line along her stomach from the curve of her breasts down towards the waistband of her briefs. His touch was feathery and light and sinful in all that it didn't do.

'I thought you warned me against complications when I first landed on your doorstep.' Miranda laughed huskily.

'So I did,' he agreed. Then his finger trailed a path lower to feel the swollen folds of her womanhood pressing against the fabric of her underwear and she groaned. She wasn't sure whether her feet were going to continue to support her and it had nothing to do with the remnants of a sprain! Her hands were desperate to drag down the thin covering which was the only barrier left between herself and this bulky man tenderly touching her, his finger moving rhythmically against her throbbing crease.

'Feel good?' he asked roughly and Miranda moaned in response.

'And how does this feel?' He replaced his finger with his mouth and nuzzled against the damp briefs, pulling her against his face with his hands from behind the rounded cheeks of her bottom. The rough lace rubbed against her and through it she could feel the prodding of his tongue. Then he brought his thumbs around her thighs and slipped them under the elasticated edges of the briefs, ruffling them into the silky hair that enclosed her pulsating womanhood.

Hooking his fingers under the waistband he gently drew her underwear down until she was standing in front of him fully naked, her shallow, rapid breathing making her full breasts rise and fall. She wanted his mouth back there, licking her, rousing her, but he sat back and studied her with a little smile of satisfaction playing around the corners of his mouth.

'Bend over me,' he commanded roughly, 'I haven't even begun tasting you yet, my darling.'

Miranda leaned over him, balancing with her hands on the back of the chair, on either side of his head, so that her breasts dangled tantalisingly in front of his mouth, and he adjusted his body accordingly to catch one dangling nipple in his mouth, suckling on it while his hand toyed with the other hanging breast, rubbing the deep pink nipple with the rough pad of his thumb.

Miranda wanted to scream in ecstasy. He wanted to take his time. He wasn't going to rush anything and she had to force herself to move to his rhythm, even though she was aching to climax.

He let her breasts hang as he licked the deep cleavage with his tongue, then moved to concentrate on her other nipple, sucking and nibbling on it.

The tight bud in the centre of its pink halo was hard and erect and he teased it mercilessly with his mouth and tongue. When she could stand it no longer, Miranda climbed onto his lap, squatting on him so that she could feel, beneath his trousers, his own big erection, pushing against his zip.

'Aren't you going to get out of your clothes?' she questioned urgently.

'In my own good time. You did say you wanted me to take charge, didn't you?'

Miranda nodded.

'I thought so. Lean back. Let me continue with your beautiful breasts.'

Instead of leaning back, she cupped both her breasts in her hands, pushing them up so that the nipples appeared even bigger and more swollen than they were. The pink circles drooped over her fingers and their eyes met as he slowly rubbed the tips with his fingers. They looked at each other, enjoying watching each other's reactions. Making love had never been this explosive. She felt as though someone had struck a match to her, and responses she had never known existed had been ignited.

She wondered whether he was feeling the same thing too, but she wouldn't ask.

He leaned forward and licked her nipple, and Miranda placed her hand behind his head, so that she was pushing him against her with one hand, while the other hand continued to offer him the bounty of her breast, feeding it to him like ripe fruit.

As he sucked her sensitised nipple, she felt his hand cup her between her thighs and she began to move sinuously against his fingers, making soft grunting noises of pleasure as her own tight, female erection brushed against his hands.

She reached behind her and clumsily tried to undo the button of his trousers, desperate to feel him, flesh against flesh, desire pressing against desire.

'Do you want me as much as I want you?' she whispered huskily.

'Can't you feel it?'

'Not enough.'

'Then we'd better set that straight, hadn't we?' He lifted her off him and she watched in open fascination as he removed his shirt and then stood up, gloriously masculine, to shed himself of the rest of his clothing.

He was magnificent. In the subdued light of the room, his torso gleamed with the hard perfection of a fighter's, and when he pulled down his boxer shorts, his manhood rose, proudly claiming his own hunger for her.

He stood in front of her and held her head between his hands, guiding her to it. She felt his big body shudder and he flung his head back with a deep groan of satisfaction, as her mouth circled his powerful erection.

She could bring him to the brink as quickly as he had brought her, she realised with a spurt of pleasure. She licked and sucked until he could stand it no longer and eased himself reluctantly away from the source of pleasure.

'It's a bit cramped here for what I want to do to you,' he murmured and Miranda laughed in thrilled anticipation.

'Shall we go upstairs?' she asked softly.

'I don't promise I can make it that far without taking you on the way,' Luke growled and she laughed again with full-bodied enjoyment at his blatant need. It matched hers.

There was a battered pine chest in the corner of the room, and she watched, sliding her body over the chair in abandonment, as he lifted the lid and extracted a downy quilt which he spread in front of the fire.

'Come and lie down,' he told her. Miranda walked towards him, loving the way his eyes devoured her every movement. He was as single-minded and focused in this as he appeared to be in everything else, and she felt intensely desirable. She lay down and he towered over her, then he straddled her, his knees on either side of her slender hips.

'Lie spread-eagled for me, darling,' he murmured, and she practically purred with heady compliance as she stretched her arms above her head and opened her legs.

'Now, let me pleasure you.' He bent to kiss her lips, her closed eyes, the slim column of her neck. He licked her breasts, his tongue flicking erotically over her prominent nipples, which were dark with arousal. Then he worked his way slowly downwards until his dark head lay between her opened legs and this time there was no lacy barrier to contain the sensation of his tongue against her slippery heat. With his hands on her thighs, making sure that her legs were spread wide for his enjoyment, he licked and sucked and rolled his tongue over her female arousal, flicking against the bud until she writhed and arched with convulsions.

Only when he knew that she could stand it no longer, did he insert himself into her, thrusting powerfully, bringing them both to a shuddering climax and then continuing until wave after wave of pleasure finally melted into blissful fulfilment.

Miranda, exhausted, dozed against him, her body curling into his and fitting into his contours like a hand in a glove. She had no idea how long she would have continued dozing in her contented, dreamy state, if the shrill ring of his mobile phone hadn't jerked her back to reality.

Luke groaned and fumbled around on the sofa with one hand for the phone, finally sitting up and answering it while Miranda twisted around and stroked his stomach with her fingers.

'Yes,' she heard him say down the phone. 'Absolutely fine. Yes. In fact, she's just here. She went outside for the first time today and…' he shot her a wicked, amused smile '…she seems thoroughly exhausted at the exertion.'

He handed her the phone and her father's voice boomed down the end of the line.

'I hope you haven't been overdoing things,' her father admonished, and she tried not to burst out laughing as she caught Luke's gaze and held it. 'You've got to take it easy with that ankle of yours. I know you told me it's all healed up but you don't want to do anything stupid and jeopardise progress.'

'I wouldn't dream of doing anything stupid, Dad.' She watched as Luke settled back down next to her, lying on his side so that he could play with her breast. Miranda smacked his hand lightly and made pointing motions to the phone, which he ignored.

'Pretty much cleared,' she said, in answer to her father's question about the snow. 'Yes. Yes. I'll let you know later…yes. All right. Bye for now. I love you, too.'

Luke removed the phone from her hands and replaced it on the sofa, then he looked at her with a teasing expression.

'So…you wouldn't dream of doing anything stupid…' He laughed and stroked her hair away from her face, propping himself up on his elbow so that he could stare down at her face which was still flushed in the aftermath of their lovemaking.

'Now, I wonder what your father's definition of stupid would be if he knew what his call had just interrupted…'

'Do you think I've been stupid?' she asked anxiously, frowning.

'You mean, do I think *we've* been stupid…? Quite possibly.' He kissed her very gently on her lips but Miranda was too intent on sifting through her emotions to return the kiss. She wriggled onto her elbow so that they were looking at each other on the same level.

'Why do you say that?'

'Sex tends to have repercussions,' he said, sliding his hand along her side to where her waist dipped. 'You're not a child. You know that. Maybe this poor caretaker might start having unhealthy ambitions to have a woman share his cabin with him during those long winter days, now that you've shown me how delightful female company can be...' His hand moved to trace a path along her belly and up to the crease beneath her breasts, showing her precisely what aspect of female company he considered so delightful.

She noticed that he had not specified that he wanted to have *her* as his female company, but who could blame him? She had offered herself to him, no strings attached and, like any red-blooded male, he had accepted the offer. So why should she feel this dull panic because what had been so earth-shattering for her had been commonplace for him?

She took a few steadying breaths to combat the uncomfortable feeling that her life ahead was dawning like a huge, gaping black hole and sternly told herself that everything would be different once she returned to England and left him behind. That was the way it went with holiday romances, and what they had couldn't even be called a romance.

'Dad wants to know when he can expect me back home,' Miranda said. He had been *her* one night stand and she was determined that he wouldn't forget that. Nor that he would imagine that she wanted anything beyond that. She would be the fluffy, self-centre airhead he thought she was and, when she left, she would make it absolutely clear that sex with him had not torn her world apart.

'And what will you tell him?'

'Oh…that he can expect me in a couple of days, when I know for sure that the snow isn't going to turn into another blizzard and that I can ski down to safety.'

'To safety…? Interesting word. Don't you feel safe here with me?' He nuzzled her ear and she squirmed.

'Where's the nearest town?' she asked breathlessly, and he paused.

'About a kilometre away, as the crow flies. In skiing time, no distance at all. When the weather permits, I get my provisions there if I need any, then catch the closest cable car back up and ski the distance to the cabin.'

'You ski with carrier bags in your hands? Must be a bit awkward.'

'I don't usually buy carrier bags full of provisions,' he countered, grinning. 'I buy just enough to shove in my backpack, not that I couldn't manage with ten carrier bags. I'm a very proficient skier as it happens. Unlike some not a million miles away from me…'

'Hang on…' Miranda became very still and cocked her head to one side. 'What's that noise?'

'What noise?'

'Sounds like…your modesty clanking out of control again.' She smirked and he repaid the insolence by kissing her so thoroughly that she only surfaced for air two minutes later.

'And do *you* think this is an act of stupidity?' His breath warmed her ear as she felt the flare of helpless attraction surge through her body once again.

'Well, I barely know you…' she murmured, clasping her hands behind her head, proffering the full vision of her breasts for him to peruse. Which he did with a grunt of satisfaction. 'And you might not believe me, but I don't go in for one-night stands...' He nibbled at her nipple, as she had known he would, and Miranda moaned in response. She could spend the rest of her life watching his dark head explore her body. She lightly ran her fingers through his black hair and followed the line of his jaw as he toyed with her nipple, teasing it with his tongue.

'For someone who doesn't go in for one-night stands...' he looked at her sideways, pausing in his exploration of her breast, '...you certainly seem to have got the hang of them pretty quickly...'

'That's because of you,' Miranda said quickly, regretting her outburst when he heaved himself up so that his face was close to hers.

'Shall I take that as a compliment?'

She shrugged. Now was the time to play it cool, she thought. A casual fling. Women did that sort of thing all of the time, and what had her past three boyfriends been but casual flings? They had lasted months rather than two days, but marriage had never been on the cards.

'I'm not sure,' she said huskily, her eyes drowsy as they met his. 'I might need a bit more to make up my mind one way or another...'

'Minx.' He laughed delightedly.

'If you can,' she murmured. 'I personally think it's a myth that men have the stamina to keep going all night...'

'Then you've never met the right man. You can feel my stamina if you like, my darling.' He blew into her ear and then delicately explored it with his tongue until she squirmed and giggled and forgot. Forgot about that dark hole waiting for her the minute she stepped foot back into the reality that had always been her life.

CHAPTER FIVE

'MIRANDA!'

Miranda's head shot up.

'What on earth is the matter with you?'

'Nothing!' She gazed down at the large breakfast which she had optimistically dished out for herself. Bacon, eggs, toast, marmalade. The toast lay limp and half eaten. The bacon and eggs were pristine and untouched and slowly congealing into an unappetising mass on the plate.

Her father was still peering at her over the rims of his slim reading glasses with his newspaper lowered.

'Why aren't you eating?' he demanded. He abandoned the newspaper altogether and afforded her the full brunt of his undivided attention. He was a tall, slender man with perfectly silver hair and blue eyes the same shade as his daughter's. Right now, he was dressed in his golfing garb. Every Saturday morning for as long as she could remember, her father vanished to the golf course where he played a round of eighteen holes with the same three friends who had been around since his roaring university days a million years ago.

'Spit it out,' he said. 'You've been moping around this house for the past week. Are you sickening for something, my girl?'

'What an antiquated phrase, Dad. *Sickening for something*. No, I'm not sickening for anything. I'm just not hungry.'

He ignored her mumbled explanation. 'And what are

you doing lurking around on a weekend? Shouldn't you be out and about with those friends of yours?'

'Actually, I'm not in the mood for those friends of mine.'

'Don't blame you. Freeloaders the lot of them. I just hope this mood of yours has nothing to do with that Freddie character, because you're well rid of him.'

Miranda gave a snort of disgust at the mere mention of any such thing. Freddie had tried contacting her twice since she had been back and she had told him, twice, that he could get lost. The second time she had added that if he contacted her again she would hang up and she would carry on hanging up until he got the message. For good measure, she had given him a pithy description of what she thought of him, which included the words waste of space, charmless, shallow and in dire need of some growing-up tablets. She didn't imagine that she would be hearing from him again.

'Well, you can't spend your time hanging around. Shall I,' he asked with an unsuccessful attempt to inject delicacy in his voice, 'remind you of a certain design course you took a few years ago?' He removed his specs, snapped them into their case and stuck the case in the top pocket of his shirt, then he stood up and began putting on his golfing jumper: a pale yellow affair with a navy and white diamond pattern and a discreet golfing motto embroidered on one side. 'Perhaps,' he continued, 'you're sickening for a spot of hard work for a change.'

'Why do I detect a certain smugness in your voice when you say that, Dad?' Miranda asked and he chuckled at her. 'I wouldn't know where to begin,' she added.

'I could put the word about at the golf club. Some of those wives seem to spend all their time remodelling their houses. No sooner have they done the whole place top to bottom, than they decide that it's time for a change. And, after they've done that five times, they're ready to move. Can't understand it myself.'

'I can put my own word about.' The task of doing any such thing seemed bigger and more insuperable than a hike up Mount Everest with only a backpack and a pair of walking shoes. Just the thought of it sent her scuttling into a state of panic. Where would she start? An advert in the newspaper? Or at the back of one of those home magazines? Or would she be reduced to standing at the corner of Sloane Square handing out leaflets in the freezing rain? Maybe wearing one of those sandwich boards with the heading, I Haven't Done This For Years, But Please Give Me A Chance.

She would think about it, she decided, next week. Right now, there were more pressing things to think about.

As soon as the house was empty, Miranda wandered aimlessly into the snug, sprawled down on the sofa, closed her eyes and reawakened the memories that were constantly gnawing away at the back of her mind and which coalesced into the haunting vision of Luke Decroix. She gave her mind free rein to travel down roads that she knew would end up hurting her. In fact, she took almost a sadistic delight in wallowing undisturbed in her self-pity.

Her last day at the cabin had dawned with a sense of glorious excitement. They had spent the night making love or at least it had felt that way. In fact, it had been as if time had stood still for them, giving them an eternity in which to explore each other's bodies, and explore them they had. She had touched every part of him, delighting in the feel of his muscled chest, the straining power of his broad shoulders, the girth of his aroused manhood that pulsed between her hands and against her mouth.

And he had caressed every inch of her body, from her

face to her feet, making her spread herself out for him so that he could rifle every part of her.

She had awakened on her final morning with the sun streaming in through the window and the feeling that she had been having the most wonderful dream: a dream about her dark, exciting lover that had left her warm and drowsily aroused.

When she'd turned around and had sleepily opened her eyes, she'd found herself staring into his alert and wide awake ones.

'You look remarkably satisfied,' he murmured with a sultry, knowing look. 'You weren't thinking about me by any chance, were you?' He pulled down the duvet cover so that her pink nipple peeked out at him. 'Oh, yes, I see that you were...'

'What time is it?' She snuggled comfortably into the feathery mattress of his king-sized bed and stretched, arching her arms above her head so that the quilt was pushed further down. When she relaxed, she made no move to re-cover her body and her breasts pointed wickedly at him. She had never felt this strange, powerful excitement at having a man look at her before. He knew how to make her feel weak with craving before he even laid one finger on her.

'Does it matter? I think we should forget about watches today and just make our own timetable up as we go along.'

'Does that mean stay in bed all day?'

'Not *all* day, no...' He blew on her nipple and the rush of cool air further hardened the tight peak and made her sigh with pleasure. 'But mornings are special, don't you agree? Why rush this one when we can laze here for a bit and...' he blew on her nipple again and she dreamily responded with a soft moan that brought a devilish smile to his mouth '…chat…'

'What do you want to chat about?'

'Anything that takes your fancy, my darling…' At which he smoothed his hand along her thighs, still warm and luxuriantly pliable from sleep, thereby ensuring that chat became the very last thing she wanted to do. Or was even capable of doing for that matter.

'Don't mind me,' he said softly, 'I'm listening to every word you're saying.' He gave her a smattering of tiny pecks around her mouth, then proceeded to kiss her thoroughly and devastatingly before turning his attention to her breasts. He pushed her so that she was lying on her back, and began suckling on her breasts, enveloping her warm nipples in his mouth.

'What…are we going…?' Miranda gave a long groan of satisfaction as more than one part of her body was stimulated by his fingers and his mouth simultaneously. She dropped her knees to either side so that he could rub his big hand against her, taking her to dizzy heights of sensation before slowing his tempo to allow her to subside, only to recommence his assault on her senses.

'You were saying?' he queried earnestly, glancing up from her breast briefly.

'To do today?' she managed to struggle out before his mouth travelled possessively down the flat planes of her stomach to the slippery heat that told of her burning arousal.

'Why, it's your turn to fulfil your side of the deal,' he said, 'and look after my needs for the day. And I mean,' he growled, '*all* my needs.'

The day was bright and clear, one of those days where one felt that one might just be able to see to the other side of the world and everything seemed to be in Technicolor.

It was nearer lunch-time by the time they finally descended the short flight of stairs and, still flushed from their languid lovemaking, Miranda bustled around the kitchen, enjoying herself as he watched from a kitchen chair and talked to her about some of the more remote places he had been, making her own travel anecdotes seem puny in comparison.

Her eyes widened at tales of sights in the Far East, the wilds of Canada, even China.

'Are you sure you're not making this up as you go along?' she teased. 'I can't believe you would eat sheep's eyes and insects.'

'When in Rome you do as the Romans do.' He shrugged and smiled at her expression of incredulity. 'It's a wise man who knows how to respect the beliefs and culture of others. Which is why, incidentally, you're doing the cooking. You're doing as the Romans do when in Rome.'

Miranda served a lunch of whatever could be successfully stir-fried and was amazed to find that it tasted fairly good.

She had never felt the slightest enthusiasm for anything culinary, and the lack had always been one of her father's bugbears. Her mother had loved to cook, had devoured cookery books, delighting in experimenting, and Miranda had accredited her father's ideas on women in the kitchen as old-fashioned notions which, she had never failed to tell him, were out of place in the twenty-first century. The truth, though, she uneasily recognised now, was that cooking, like her interior design, like a thousand other things over the years, had just been one more thing that she had abandoned because she lacked the perseverance to see it through.

When, over lunch, she haltingly tried to explain this to

Luke, she found that his reaction was one of sympathy rather than the so-what-was-new attitude she might have expected when she had first stumbled into his life.

'If you can see what you're dissatisfied with in your life,' he said, calling her over to him and then sitting her on his lap like a ten-year-old child in need of comfort, 'then why don't you do something about it when you get back to England?' He stroked her hair and she laid her head on his shoulder, feeling safe, the way she had when she'd been a kid and her father had patiently sat her on *his* lap and had soothed away her childish worries.

'I can't.'

'Why not?'

'Because…'

'Because you're afraid?' he persisted gently. 'Afraid of failing? I know, I know…' He carried on stroking her hair, soothing her, and she realised that he understood everything, things she had never vocalised to anyone before, not even to her father. 'It's easier to succeed at being a beautiful young thing without a care in the world than to allow the world to judge you on your merits.'

His voice, as he continued to dissect her innermost thoughts, was like a wave washing around her, absorbing her, and she had to control the temptation not to burst out crying.

She only had the remainder of this day left! She sat up and sighed but, before she could move away, he pulled her back against him, this time to kiss her with a tenderness that made her weak.

Kissing him was what she needed. She didn't need to think and analyse and end up feeling maudlin! She took his tender kiss and returned it fiercely, her tongue clashing with his. With a lithe manoeuvre, she straddled him, rolling her hips provocatively and pushing him back into his chair with her mouth still possessing his. Right now, all she wanted was to lose herself in his lovemaking because, when she left this cabin, he would be gone for ever and all she would have left would be her memories and an uncomfortable awareness that she would have to start sorting her life out.

'No!' she whispered, when he tried to lift her out towards the sitting room.

'You certainly are taking me to my word about satisfying my needs,' he groaned into her ear and she felt the savage pull of satisfaction at her power over him. Right now. Right at this instant. Tomorrow could wait...

Miranda gave a soft moan of despair as she stared upwards at the ceiling in her father's house.

Playing back the scene of their lovemaking in her head was like watching a film in slow motion. If it had ended there, then she would still be staring at the ceiling in her father's house, she thought, but at least she would have had her dignity intact.

Instead, his little words about not being afraid of failing had somehow wormed their way into her head and had taken root. That, combined with the crippling prospect of never seeing him again, had made her utter something she should have held to herself. Cradling his head against her as they had collapsed, spent after their raw lovemaking, she had asked him if he'd wanted her to stay.

'Just for a few days,' she said hastily and, when his response was not immediate, she sat up and gazed down into his eyes.

'It wouldn't be a good idea,' he told her finally. 'You can't grab a bit of time to hide away here so that you won't have to face whatever you feel you have to face when you return to England.'

His rejection of her offer hit her like a sledgehammer,

but she remained in control of her feelings, willing herself not to shrivel up under those cobalt eyes.

He didn't want her. He had been content to sleep with her because she had offered herself to him, but the bottom line was that he just didn't want her. She wasn't his type and prolonging her stay, far from being a pleasurable prospect for him, was the offer of just a little too much of a good thing.

Who knew, maybe he had even got a kick out of sleeping with a woman who was so far removed from the type of earthy woman he was probably accustomed to. Like sleeping with the boss's daughter: an illicit thrill but not one to be stretched out and with limited novelty value.

'You understand what I'm saying, don't you, Miranda?' he asked and she nodded obligingly, not allowing herself to speak for fear of doing something ridiculous.

'I wasn't talking about commitment and marriage.' She finally found her voice and used it, embarking on a damage-limitation exercise even though her heart, her dignity, her pride were all breaking into a thousand pieces.

'I know that,' he told her impatiently, following her to the bathroom so that he could pursue the conversation to her back.

'I just thought it might have been fun.' She washed, aware of his eyes burning a hole through her but unable to find any excuse to request privacy after they had jettisoned any such notion along the way. To suddenly ask to be alone would be tantamount to telling him how devastated she was by what he was saying.

'But you're right.' She even found the strength from somewhere to give a brittle laugh, though she couldn't meet his eyes. They saw altogether too much. 'It's best to call it a day. Bit of fun but familiarity breeds contempt, or so they say.'

She changed into her original ski gear and had then to undergo the gauntlet of having him ski down with her to the nearest village, which as he had told her, was only a hop and a skip away. Then he waited. Waited so that they could have a cup of coffee until the cable car was ready to take her down to the final stop where a taxi would speed her to the airport and away from him for ever.

And there had been more questions. More shows of sympathy that made her want to scream. And finally she was gone, gone without a backward glance. Just a casual wave to imply that it had all been a bit of a laugh and have a good life.

Miranda wearily sat up and stretched. Her father would be back from his golfing expedition in a couple of hours and it wouldn't do to have him find her skulking around the house like a lost soul. He might not have much experience of honing into women's emotions but he was astute and it wouldn't take him much longer to figure out the reason for her inexplicable lack of energy.

At least, she consoled herself, she hadn't made the mistake of blurting out the confession that would have turned her mortification into downright agony. When she had looked at Luke, lost in his eyes, she had managed not to tell him that she had fallen in love with him.

She waited until her father returned, having changed into a long-sleeved woollen dress and tied her hair back, and greeted him with a bright smile.

'Good game?' she asked, trailing behind him into the kitchen where he began removing his shoes and socks. 'Lost many balls?'

'Since when have you been interested in your old man's golfing exploits?' He gave her a shrewd look from under bushy silver brows. 'Bloody awful game, now that you asked. Putting everywhere but the hole. Damned Gordon had a good laugh at my expense when we got to the nine-teenth hole.'

'I've decided,' she said, taking a deep breath, 'to go out to work.'

Her father paused to look at her. 'Good girl.' He padded out to the utility room where he left his shoes and, when he returned to the kitchen, he said casually, 'What brought about his sudden change of direction?'

Miranda shrugged. 'I'm fed up with doing nothing.' She looked at him and grinned. 'I'm an adult now. Perhaps I just think that the time has come to realise that adults don't spend their lives having good times. They work hard and feel miserable.'

Her father laughed and patted her head as he walked past her to the kettle. 'That's the spirit. So where are you going to begin?'

'Back at design college. I'll go along and hear what they have to say about idlers who want to relaunch their career after years of wasting time.'

'I might be able to help,' he said conversationally.

'The golfing fraternity?'

'Or some such thing. Who knows? You might find that you land on your feet quicker than you think. I mean,' he continued hastily, 'you've always had a lot of talent. Anyone just has to take a look at your portfolio to see that for themselves.'

Unfortunately, she was told the following Monday when she trotted along to the careers office at the design college, a lack of portfolio was something of a hindrance. Especially, she was advised by the impeccably groomed brunette, in a field that was so highly competitive. The time lapse also posed a problem. Were her ideas as fresh as they once had been? Fashions in interior design had moved on. Did she have any contacts at all in the field?

Another problem apparently. A refresher course, she was informed, might be worth thinking about, and Miranda left an hour and a half later with an armful of further course details.

Rather than return to the house and face a long day contemplating her lack of experience, Miranda spent the day out, reluctantly contacting one of her friends for lunch who gave her the full story about the remainder of their skiing trip and Freddie's high junks. Accounts of her own exploits she kept to a minimum. In a small circle, gossip had an unfortunate tendency to spread like wildfire and usually underwent alterations along the way so that the end story bore little resemblance to the truth. Like Chinese whispers.

By the time six-thirty rolled round, she let herself into the house feeling thoroughly beaten by the prospect of her jobless, pointless existence.

'Miranda, darling,' Her father popped out of the sitting room with a drink in one hand as she was divesting herself of her coat and wondering what to do with the lists of courses which had failed to inspire the flurry of interest anticipated by the careers advisor. It was all right for her, Miranda had thought sourly at the time, to sit there and give long lectures about the gaping holes in other peoples' curriculum vitaes, when she herself was ensconced in a nice, cosy career of her own. Perhaps she should scrap all thoughts of returning to interior design and instead try for a recruitment agency so that she could spend all her time telling people without the necessary qualifications that they didn't have the necessary qualifications.

'You're home early, Dad.' She slung her coat over the banister, a habit her father deplored, and ran her fingers through her hair. 'Don't tell me you've decided to take early retirement.'

'Successful day?'

Miranda looked at him gloomily. 'Apparently I need a bulging portfolio, a load of contacts and neither would help anyway because I've been out of the field for so long that all my ideas are outdated and in dire need of a spring-clean.' She waved the course details at him. 'I could always do a refresher course, I'm told, but even then it's such a competitive field that I probably wouldn't get anywhere anyway.'

'Well,' he gave her a long, satisfied look, 'I might just have the answer for you, my girl.'

'What's that, Dad? A position in one of your companies? Or maybe you could let me redecorate your office. It would be a start and I offer hefty discounts to family members.' She grinned. 'I've always thought that hose browns and beiges in your office are a bit on the fuddy-duddy side.'

'Join me in the sitting room for a drink.' He winked at her and spun round on his heels with his daughter tramping behind him. 'And it doesn't,' he threw over his shoulder, 'involve getting rid of my nice browns and beiges.'

'Oh, yes? What does it involve?'

Instead of answering, her father stood back and made a sweeping gesture from the door of the sitting room, allowing her to enter ahead of him.

Miranda, about to continue her speculations about alternative job prospects, stopped in mid-track, with her mouth half open and the ghost of a smile rapidly dying on her lips.

What the hell was *he* doing here? What was Luke Decroix doing in her father's house, sitting in one of her father's chairs, with a drink casually in one hand, the other resting on the arm of his chair?

Miranda blinked rapidly as the air was squeezed out of

her lungs by this sudden apparition who was now raising
his drink to his lips and wore the easy self-assurance of
someone who feels utterly at home.

In her father's house!

'I believe you two know one another,' her father said
from behind her and her wildly spiralling thoughts con-
verged with crashing awareness that this was no illusion.

Luke Decroix, for reasons unknown to her, had left his
caretaking job and had dogged her back to England.

'What can I get you to drink, darling?' her father bustled past her, looking suspiciously pleased with himself
and oblivious to her rising panic.

'Water!' Miranda gasped, then she took control of herself and cleared her throat. 'On second thoughts, a glass
of white wine, Dad. Thanks.'

'So, we meet again.' Luke, who had followed her stum-
bling progress from doorway to sofa, smiled and raised
his glass in mimicry of an old friend. Miranda felt like
choking.

'Look at you,' her father said affectionately, thrusting
the wineglass into her hand, 'aren't you thrilled?'

'Speechless,' she managed to choke out, before swallowing a generous mouthful of the cold liquid in a mis-
guided attempt to clear her head.

'You do look a bit white, if anything,' Luke said drily.
He placed his drink carefully on the polished side table
and then loosely linked his fingers together on his lap so
that he could give her his undivided attention.

'She's had a bit of a day, from the sounds of it,' her
father was saying. 'No wonder the poor girl's white like
a sheet. Got a bee in her bonnet about going out to work.'

'Dad, I have not got a *bee in my bonnet*. I'm just giving
it some thought.' Out of the corner of her eye, she could
see Luke looking at her with a shuttered expression.

Probably trying hard not to smirk, she thought a little wildly.

'That little stay in your cabin must have brought her to her senses.'

His cabin? She opened her mouth to put her father straight on that little point but, before she could utter a word, Luke had smoothly entered the conversation and was suborning her father with a long, philosophical spiel on isolation sometimes being the best cure, giving time to really think about what one wanted to do with oneself, affording the invaluable opportunity to get perspectives right. And her poor father was lapping it all up.

'So what brings you here?' She finally interrupted the monologue on the virtues of isolation.

'Boring you, am I?' Luke asked with a smooth, cutting edge in his voice.

'Not at all. I just wondered what you were doing over here when you should be in France. I mean, what's your er...'

'So not much luck on the job-hunting front? It's a competitive field.'

'I already know that,' Miranda snapped, while her father pointedly cleared his throat to remind his daughter about the rules of courtesy. 'I spent two hours being told it by a supercilious careers advisor. I don't need *you* to launch another sermon on the impossibility of finding work in an overcrowded field. And you still haven't answered my question.'

What would her father be thinking about him? she wondered. He had shown, oddly, very little curiosity about details of her rescuer and her own sketchy descriptions had led him down the road of a thoroughly nice man, by which she had tacitly implied that he was genial and middle-aged.

What would he be thinking at the strikingly good-looking man sitting on his chair, with a faint air of aggression about him? Or maybe Luke had spent however long he had been in the house, inveigling his way into her father's good books so that unanswerable questions about his prized daughter being in the company for a period of days with a man who would turn heads with the best of them, were stillborn. God knew, he seemed to be bringing out the charm in plentiful supply.

'I'm here to help you, actually.' Luke smiled blandly as she tried to work out what precisely he meant by that. He tapped a briefcase which she noticed for the first time was upright on the ground next to his chair.

'Perhaps I should let you two young people discuss this on your own.' He stood to rise and Miranda practically yelled at him to stay put.

'There's nothing that can't be said in front of my father!' she declared on a shout. The thought of being left alone in the room with Luke brought her out in a cold sweat. He had used her, she decided, conveniently forgetting any thoughts that she had led him on. On the back of this, she felt a satisfying rush of antagonism.

Had he come back to *help her* by asking her whether her offer of a bit more uncomplicated sex was still on the agenda? What a nerve! To brazenly come to her house, cosy up to her father and then try and pretend to him that he was actually on a mission to *help*? Miranda felt a bubble of manic laughter at the back of her throat and swallowed it down.

'Luke's come to see you on business,' her father said. 'Now, I might run a number of companies but when it comes to discussing interior design, well, I'm lost.' He beamed at Luke. 'As this little snippet of a thing will be the first to tell you!'

'Is that right, you little snippet of a thing?' He glanced up from his briefcase, from which he had successfully extracted a sheaf of papers. Miranda, who had been watching his activities in open-mouthed silence, snapped her teeth together.

'Why have you got a briefcase?'

'Now, you *will* be polite, won't you, Miranda?' her father said in a warning voice, and she gave him a pitying glance, willing him to read her mind, that whatever nefarious tale Luke Decroix had spun, it was all a lie.

'Oh, I know how to handle your daughter,' Luke said drily, and she caught the double meaning behind his words and felt a rush of colour sting her cheeks.

'Now, young man, how about a spot of dinner when you're through here?'

Miranda gaped but, before she could squawk out her thoughts on any such idea, Luke was nodding his acceptance and making some crack about bringing a bottle of wine if he had known that he would be staying for dinner.

'Sure you haven't got anything else planned?' Her father turned at the door to look at them. He belonged to an era whose idea of casual dress meant no tie or jacket and he looked well-dressed enough to go out in his grey slacks, smart shoes and blue shirt the top button of which he had daringly left undone. Miranda felt a wave of pure love engulf her and her silent rage that this imposter could try and dupe her beloved father made her head feel as if it was going to explode.

'Nothing that can't be put on hold,' Luke was saying, his voice warmly appreciative of the offer.

'Do you mind telling me what's going on here?' Miranda demanded as soon as her father had left the sitting room, tactfully closing the door behind him. 'How *dare* you talk your way into my father's house on some phoney pretext! *How dare you?*' Her hands gripped the edge of the sofa, biting into the cushion.

'You don't seem too pleased to see me,' Luke countered lazily. 'Why not?' His eyes flicked over her flushed face then took in her prim powder-blue suit and blue pumps, the garb she had foolishly imagined would have suited her first day back on the job-seeking front. 'After all we shared... Still, I understand. It's always a bit disconcerting when two separate strands of reality collide.'

'How did you know where to find me?'

'I telephoned your father.'

'And wangled your way into his house by telling him what...?'

'By telling him that I have a little job for you to do.'

Miranda gave a cackle of disbelieving laughter. 'Well, he'll soon realise that whatever little job you might have is all in your head when I let him know who and what you really are!' Actually, seeing Luke there, feet away from her, inspired hysteria. It also revived the bitter taste of his rejection. She bit back the temptation to shriek with demented laughter and lunge for his neck with something very sharp in her hand.

He, she noted, looked perfectly at ease in his surroundings and unfazed by the fact that she was about to uncover his duplicity.

'Why do you think I've come here, then, Miranda?'

'Maybe you think you can somehow get money from my father,' she said callously. 'I don't know, you tell me.'

'What are these?' He handed her the papers he had been holding but, instead of taking them, Miranda just peered at the top one.

'Those are my designs for your boss's house.' She looked at him sharply. 'Why have you got them? I thought you'd deleted them from the computer. What's going on here?' The hostility in her voice was laced with genuine confusion. 'Does your boss know what you're up to?'

'Ah.' Luke dropped the papers on the ground and sat back to look at her. 'It's time you and I had a little chat.'

CHAPTER SIX

MIRANDA drank some of her wine, a taste for which she seemed to have developed ever since her stay in the cabin, and eased her feet out of her pumps. It was imperative that she take the upper hand and not let Luke Decroix try and manoeuvre her in her own home territory. But, when she stretched out to place her wineglass on the table in front of her, she found that her hand was trembling and she hurriedly folded her arms across her chest and looked at him coldly.

'Why,' she asked in a controlled voice, 'are you here *really*? What are you doing with my designs? And what have you told my father?'

'Which question do you want me to answer first?'

'I don't care. Just so long as you answer all of them and then get out of my father's house and out of my life.'

Instead of answering, though, Luke sat back in his chair and contemplated her over the rim of his glass. He took a leisurely sip of his drink, carefully placed his glass on the table next to him and then linked his fingers together on his lap, rubbing the pads of his thumbs together.

In the ensuing silence, Miranda had a good chance to look at him and to notice that his clothes bore no resemblance to the old gear he had worn in the cabin. In fact, he looked smart. Expensively smart. The trousers were hand-tailored, the crisp blue and white shirt bore the hallmarks of quality as did the deep tan brogues. But then, she considered feverishly, he would have dressed up to visit her father if his aim was to try and con money out of him or at least show him a respectable side if he was harbouring some dark hidden agenda.

'I didn't tell your father about us,' he said abruptly.

'There *is* no *us*!'

'Okay, I'll rephrase that. I didn't tell your father that the apple of his eye had made a play for the caretaker and embarked on a passionate, two-day fling, no strings attached. I didn't think that particular version of the truth would be appropriate.'

Miranda glanced nervously over her shoulder just in case her father was hovering. 'I did not...'

'Oh, yes, you did. But don't worry. That's still our little secret.'

Still? Did that mean that he intended to spill the beans if she didn't go along with whatever he had in mind? Her cheeks were flushed with hectic colour. 'If you've come here to blackmail me...' she whispered urgently, leaning forward and impatiently pushing her hair away from her face.

'What would you do about it?' He looked at her coldly.

'It would be your word against mine!'

'Well, I'll just set your seedy little mind at rest by telling you that I don't play those kinds of games. In case you're interested, I have a lot of respect for your father...'

'Having never seen him in your life before!' Miranda burst out shrilly. She snatched the drink from the table and shakily drank some more of her wine in an attempt to steady her nerves.

'That's not quite true.'

It took several seconds for that simple sentence to find its way to her brain and several more for it to gather momentum. Miranda stared at the man sitting opposite her. She was dreaming all of this. In a minute, she would wake up and discover that, in fact, she was still crushed in between two overweight businessmen on the Underground and had in fact nodded off and had begun having a wild, inexplicable dream. She blinked.

'What do you mean? What are you talking about?'

'It means...' He shook his head and then began restlessly prowling through the room, pausing to examine various *objets d'art*, although Miranda got the impression that he wasn't so much looking at them as giving himself time to think.

Finally he returned to his chair but, instead of sitting down, he perched on the fat, cushioned arm of the chair, his long legs extended in front of him. 'I know your father, Miranda. I've met him a number of times before.'

'You're lying.'

'I know you find what I'm saying hard to believe but...'

'You're lying. Why are you lying to me? What are you trying to prove?'

'I'm not trying to prove anything!' he said impatiently. 'Just listen to what I'm going to tell you without interrupting. You can save your thoughts for later.' He raked his fingers through his hair and glanced at her. Under normal circumstances, Miranda would have enjoyed seeing this big, powerful, self-assured man floundering but her mind was too involved along its own tricky path to appreciate his rare failure to be in command.

'When you showed up at my cabin...'

'*Your* cabin?'

Luke shot her another impatient look. 'That's right. *My* cabin.'

'But you said...'

'I suppose it was too much asking you to sit out my explanation in silence. Yes, yes, I know what I said.' He resumed his prowling until she could feel her nerves being shredded by his ceaseless movement.

'I wish you'd just sit down and tell me what you have to tell me!' she snapped, and he gave a little shrug of his shoulders, obediently sitting down, though unfortunately on the sofa alongside her. She sat panic-stricken, frozen on the sofa.

'I didn't actually tell you that I was a caretaker,' he said slowly, 'I just agreed with what you assumed.'

'Why would you do that? None of this makes any sense.' Miranda shook her head in utter bewilderment, hoping to catch a glimmer of revelation and failing. She felt like someone trying to find the way out of a labyrinth with every turn leading to a dead end.

'Why would I do that…?' he murmured, looking at her. 'The fact is I own the cabin. I know I told you it wasn't mine, but it is. It's my bolt-hole. Every year for three weeks I disappear there to wind down from the stresses of my daily life. I take time out. I see no one because I invite no one there to see me. So you can well imagine my annoyance when you interrupted my solitude with your sprained ankle and your expensive, well-bred, pathetic helplessness.'

Miranda was still trying to imagine this man being the owner of the cabin, never mind picture what he'd felt when she'd stumbled into him. Her brain had not quite made it to that particular point of the narration as yet.

'So what do you do?' she asked in a dazed voice.

'I work in London, as it happens.'

'You work in London.' She might have been saying, so you live on Planet Mars.

'I thought that it was just typical of a girl like you to assume that a man like me, holed up in a basic little cabin far from the glamour of the ski slopes, couldn't possibly be anything more than a poor, lowly caretaker and, I admit, I found the assumption amusing. Amusing and con-

venient. I had no desire to find myself at the receiving
end of some impressionable little girl fresh out of a relationship and on the lookout for another rich man to en-
snare.'

Miranda felt her cheeks sting and she rested her head
in the palms of her hands. 'You lied to me.'

'Look at me.' He gently circled one of her wrists with
his fingers and she flinched as though she had been burnt.
Flinched and pulled away, shifting further up the sofa. But
she did look at him.

'I admit, it suited me. Then you told me your name and
I realised that I knew your father. Didn't it ever occur to
you that your father was singularly unworried by you being trapped in the middle of nowhere with a stranger?'

'I thought…I thought that even if he was worried, he
would be more relieved by the fact that I was safe.'

'Of course he was relieved that you were safe. He was
also infinitely more relieved that you had had the luck to
be saved by someone he knew personally.'

'I would have met you…'

'No, Miranda.' He shook his head gently. 'Your life
and your father's business life barely touched. I'd bet my
life that you wouldn't recognise ninety per cent of the
people he mixes with through business.'

It was true. When she'd been younger, he had tried to
encourage her to play the occasional hostess at some of
his corporate events but, after the first one, she had declared herself bored with the concept of having to make
polite conversation with people who'd meant nothing to
her, and he had never pressed her again.

'And one of those people was me. To cut a long story
short, years ago, he helped raise the finance to get my
father's business on the road and, from that point on, he
remained friends with my father. Despite the fact that your

father was born into wealth, he was still imbued with the values of hard work and making his way in the world through his own efforts. He could appreciate similar aspirations in my father. Much later, I wanted some advice on a takeover I was planning and I consulted your father.'

The storyline was getting so complicated that her brain was finding it hard to keep up.

'So Dad and you had a cosy little chat about me and then what…? Decided that I ought to remain ignorant of your true identity? How could he? How could *you*?' She felt tears of mortification sting the backs of her eyes.

'It wasn't quite like that,' Luke said mildly. 'I spoke to your father on the telephone…'

'I remember. You went into the kitchen to do that…'

'I told him that you were with me and made some joke about the fact that you thought I was the hired help; and, after we had laughed a bit about it, he suggested that it might be an idea to go along with the assumption because a bit of hard work might do you the world of good. I agreed.'

'A bit of hard work!'

'Try not to fly off the handle, Miranda,' Luke said sharply. 'Just take a minute to look at yourself from the outside. You've lived a life of privilege, doted on by your father. I doubt you've ever come across anyone who hasn't automatically fallen in line with what you want. Believe me, your father didn't have to twist my arm to go along with his idea. I was one hundred per cent behind it. I thought it would do you the world of good not to have your own way for once. I also had no intention of pandering to a rich young girl's every whim.'

'And letting me play around on your computer was what? Another kindly piece of education to guide me in the right direction? One more addition to your little experiment?' Her voice was laced with bitterness.

'Actually,' Luke said drily, 'I thought it would give you something to do. I remember your father telling me that you were talented and I was curious to see what you could do.'

'And of course,' Miranda said slowly, 'I was working on *your* house, wasn't I?'

'My house.' He agreed.

'And making love?' she blurted out. 'What was that? More home tutoring in how to make wilful Miranda into a more responsible adult?' She clenched her fists and fought down a feeling of nausea.

'That was...' His face flushed darkly. 'That was... unexpected.'

'And should I be flattered by that?' she threw at him. 'That it wasn't part of your grand, master plan?'

'There was no master plan.'

Miranda gave a snort of incredulous laughter that verged on sobbing.

'Stop being so damned selfish,' he grated. 'Your father thought it might be a much needed experience. To understand what it was like to cook for yourself, amuse yourself, do all the millions of things that you have never had any need to do for yourself.

'Now, you may like to take the moral high ground and think that you were somehow betrayed, but let's take a good, close look at it. You've come back to England and you haven't been able to feel too happy about resuming your normal existence, have you?'

His voice was brutal. If she could have fled to another part of the house, then she would have, but she suspected that any thoughts of escape would be well and truly cut off by the man skewering her with his eyes. And she knew from experience that she wouldn't stand a chance against him when it came to flight.

'Well, have you?' he repeated harshly, barely giving her time to repair her battered defences.

'I...' She raised her blue eyes to his.

'You're looking for a job because you can't face the thought of getting back on that mad, pointless merry-go-round, can you? You're fed up with the ride, aren't you Miranda? Fed up with the same old people doing the same old things in the same old places. You've had time to think...'

'For which I should be thanking you, I suppose!'

'And you want out. Which is why you've been tramping the streets of London looking for work...'

'I have not,' Miranda informed him, clutching to the few shreds of self-composure that hadn't yet been demolished under his remorseless litany of accusations, 'been "tramping the streets of London looking for work". I've tramped to the careers advisory office at the design college.'

He shrugged dismissively as though her insistence on precision was beside the point.

This was the man she had fallen in love with! She was finding it hard to understand why, even though she knew with frightening honesty that, despite everything he had said and done, she still found herself compulsively attuned to his presence, like a drought victim with water in sight.

'Where you've been told that there's a stiff price to be paid for your years of cheerful abandon.'

'You didn't need much imagination to get to that conclusion,' Miranda said sullenly, 'considering my father announced it the minute he was in the room.'

'Are you all right?' The sudden shift in tone caught her unawares and her eyes flickered hesitantly over his face, then she stared down at her powder-blue lap, her mouth down-turned.

If he thought she was going to admit that what he had said to her or, rather, had rammed down her throat, had made sense, then he had another think coming. She felt like someone who had been unwittingly used as a guinea pig in an experiment and, even though the experiment had worked, still felt like a guinea pig.

No wonder he hadn't wanted her to stay on. The experiment had been over. It had been time for the guinea pig to head home. She felt a wave of self-pity batter the hastily erected walls of her self-control and she inhaled deeply, steadying her ragged nerves.

'Never been better,' she offered icily. 'I've just discovered that I've been the butt of a quality learning experience hatched up by you and my dad, been made love to by someone who loathed me on sight and probably still loathed me when he was making love to me but couldn't resist the free offer, and you ask me if I'm all right. Why shouldn't I be all right?'

Luke looked at her steadily through narrowed, dangerously perceptive eyes. 'Whoever mentioned anything about loathing you?' he asked in a voice that matched the expression in his eyes. 'And if your intention is to insult my intelligence by suggesting that I made love to a woman I loathed, then you've succeeded. I have never laid a finger on a woman I didn't like and I hope to God I never do.' Which was something, she thought resentfully. He *liked* her, meaningless word that it was.

But, before she could analyse what he had said, he was continuing with the same merciless intensity, 'and while you're thrashing about in the throes of self-pity and wounded pride, why don't you spare a thought for me?'

'For *you*?' She gaped incredulously at him and was

tempted to shriek with laughter. 'Why should I feel sorry for *you*?'

'Whatever motives you may credit me with for making love to you,' he told her with a thread of steel in his voice, 'your own motives are firmly rooted in some pretty murky water as well.'

Miranda's disbelieving jaw dropped a few inches further.

'There you were, perhaps not heartbroken after your little fling with the philandering Freddie, but certainly with your pride a bit on the bruised side. Consciously or subconsciously, what better way to restore some of your dented ego than a fling with a robust yokel?'

'Stop referring to yourself as a yokel,' was all she could find to refute this piece of incisive but utterly off-target logic. Trust a man to apply the forces of reason to a situation and unreasonably reach the wrong conclusion. But then, how could he begin to guess the panic that had stifled her thinking processes when she had tried to visualise leaving him behind without a backward glance?

She certainly had no intention of setting the record straight! Least of all on a stomach full of unwelcome revelations!

She decided that a change of subject was called for. Let him remain unenlightened. She pointed to the sheaf of papers, *her* designs, which had been relegated to the floor for a while. 'And so you've come to give me some work, have you? Has my father put you up to that by any chance?'

'No, he hasn't.' He retrieved the papers and resumed his unwanted proximity to her on the sofa.

'I don't need you feeling sorry for me,' Miranda informed him, before he could launch into a patronising speech about lending a helping hand. 'I didn't have much luck with the careers advisor but I'm still confident that I can get things going. I might start by working for someone else and then see where to go from there.'

'You will be working for somebody else. You'll be working for me.'

'I don't need your help!'

'Of course, there are one or two things you'll need to improve on.'

The roaring in Miranda's ears and the gut-wrenching sensation of wanting to drop through the floor melted in the face of this fresh piece of criticism. *'Improve on?'*

'There's no need to act as though it's a dirty word.' He rustled the papers on his lap and pulled out one of them. It was her detailed design for the kitchen and she noticed that bits of her work had been changed. 'You'll never get work if you rise up in arms the minute your employer tries to put some ideas forward.'

'You are not my employer!'

'I didn't care for this central island thing. It's going to take up too much space and I don't have enough to fill the cupboards anyway. It's not necessary.'

Miranda snatched the paper away from him and jabbed her finger at one side of the drawing. 'There are only cupboards on one side!' She smirked, unable to resist the opportunity to point out an error, an error *he* had made. 'On the other side, there's empty space for bar stools so you can sit and eat at the kitchen counter if you don't want the formality of sitting at a table. There's also scope for a television to be angled against the wall *there* so you can sit and eat and watch your favourite movie; that would be one involving undercover behaviour and blackmail!'

Before she could turn away and let him stew in his mistake, he had extracted another piece of paper and was drawing her attention to a range of bookshelves she had designed for his den, bombarding her with useless questions about heights and widths and informing her that she hadn't given him enough space for a work area, which was the point of the den in the first place.

'What's the point having an extensive work area if you have an office in London?' Miranda snapped, her eyes furiously scouring the paper and mentally rearranging her design to incorporate a bigger desk with concealed panelling to house filing cabinets.

'That's not the sort of objection that should be raised to a change in design. For future reference. Anyway, I intend to do a lot more work from the house and only commute to London when necessary. I'll keep my apartment on there and use it as an occasional base. And you didn't make allowances for the pool.'

This was getting ridiculous. Miranda felt herself torn between proud and haughty retreat in the face of a job offer she had no intention of taking up, and heated defence of her designs, her first for years. Her blue eyes mirrored the internal struggle and finally she felt compelled to inform him that he had never mentioned wanting a pool.

'I've decided that I want one now.'

'Well, get in touch with some pool people and have one. There's enough land to fit ten pools if you're desperate for a spot of exercise.'

'I want an indoor one.'

'It won't fit.'

'Somewhere downstairs. More of a Jacuzzi than a pool,' he mused thoughtfully. 'Murals on the walls, a couple of columns Roman-style, and a bubbling Jacuzzi so that I can relax in the evenings with a glass of champagne.'

The image was alluring enough to have her mentally

plotting the spot. She brought herself sharply back to reality and thought about the fact that she was discussing Jacuzzis with a man who she had assumed to be a relatively penniless caretaker with nothing more on his mind than his next pit stop. The penniless caretaker she had fallen in love with. The penniless caretaker who had turned out to be an Oscar-winning actor with a degree in lying.

'There's no point going through all this with me. I don't want your job.'

'Fine.'

She watched reluctantly as he stacked the papers and shoved them back into the briefcase, feeling a certain pique that he had surrendered so easily.

'Just so long as you don't object to someone else using your designs, because I thought on the whole they were remarkably good. Very imaginative. Just what I was looking for.'

Miranda stared furiously at him. 'You can't just take my work and hand it over to someone else!' she spluttered and he gave her an implacable smile, lifting his shoulders to imply that he had no problem with that and, besides, what else could he do?

'Why not?'

'Because…because it belongs to me!'

'How do you work that out?'

'And you can stop giving me that innocent, butterwouldn't-melt-in-my-mouth look! You know exactly why you can't appropriate my work!'

'As far as I know, you never mentioned anything about charging for these designs when you started them…'

'Because I didn't think they were going to be used!'

'Your father will be disappointed. But still, it can't be helped. You've got to find your own feet and if that means turning down my job, for which you would have been more than amply paid and which would have represented something pretty major to add to your portfolio, then so be it. People would have sat up and taken you seriously after a job like this, especially when they knew who the client was. I may not have made much of a mark in the glamorous world of trendy night spots and swinging clubs but my name in financial circles holds quite a bit of credence. You would have found yourself with a number of doors flung open. But there you go. You've got to take the course of action you see fit. Shall we go and join your father now and break the news to him?' He stood up and stuck his hands in his pockets, turning to look at her.

'That's right! If I'm going to get back into this design thing, then it's got to be *my* way, without help from anyone.'

'Because accepting help is something you wouldn't do in a thousand years, isn't it?' he suggested mildly, and Miranda's darkly defined eyebrows met in a frown. 'Because you've never had to expect help from any quarter. You've always been the centre of attention and you've never wanted anything badly enough to need to ask for help.'

'Because accepting help from *you* isn't something I would do in a million years.'

'Then I shall feel no compunctions about handing your work over to someone else and letting them take eventual credit for your designs. Remember *you* would have been helping *me*.'

'But I don't want to help *you*.'

Blue met blue. Although he was clearly waiting for her to stand up so that they could leave the room and join their father for supper, Miranda found that she couldn't move.

'Pride comes before a fall, Miranda,' he murmured, so softly that she had to strain to hear him. The weight of defeat settled on her shoulders like a boulder. Defeat and, she admitted grudgingly, the thrill of a challenge, the thrill of being in contact with this man again, however much he had humiliated her.

'The only reason I would accept this job is because you're using the threat of handing my work to someone else.'

He sat back down, leaning back into the arm of the sofa so that he could cross his legs, his ankle resting on his thigh and affording her the unwelcome sight of fine wool stretching against his big muscular thighs.

'And it doesn't mean that I accept how you behaved. You made a fool of me.'

'That's ridiculous.'

Miranda was not going to be drawn into an inconclusive discussion about rights and wrongs. He and her father had connived to keep her in the dark about who he really was and to teach her a lesson. However much he sat there and tried to rationalise what they had both done, it made no difference: she felt as though she had been subjected to an exercise in humiliation.

But the cards were stacked in his favour and he knew it. She *had* changed; maybe she would have changed anyway, irrespective of their interfering. She wanted to work and he held the trump card.

'But I won't mention it again. It happened and there's nothing I can do about it.' Her voice implied that she would do plenty if she could. 'I'll work for you but the arrangement is purely business.' She reached out her hand for her designs and he gave her a hooded, lazy look from under his dark lashes.

'Not so fast. What makes you think I'm going to hand over your designs before a contract is signed?'

Miranda shot him an outraged look. 'It's called trust.'

'There's no such thing in my world,' he answered lightly while he continued to scrutinise her flustered face with a closed expression. 'In my world, it's a case of survival of the fittest and you would be surprised how many reach survival status by letting other people down.'

'Yourself included, I presume?'

'You're determined to believe the worst of me, aren't you?'

'Wouldn't *you* be if you were in my shoes?' Her restless fingers played with the tassel of one of the deep burgundy cushions on the sofa, threading the silken strands of cloth together then combing them through with her short rounded nails. 'You could have told me the truth...'

'When?' he demanded heavily. 'Perhaps I wanted to, but just couldn't find the right time to do it.'

And perhaps, Miranda thought, piecing together her own jigsaw puzzle of his motivations in her head, it had just been easier to take what had been on offer in the full knowledge that he would never have to see her again and hence would never have to deal with a confrontation he found distasteful. But then he had looked at her designs and had liked them and the confrontation had become an unavoidable reality.

'What else did you lie to me about?' she asked in a small voice. 'Are you married? Do you have a girlfriend? Are those other things you found convenient and amusing to keep to yourself?'

'You know the answers to those questions, so why ask them?'

'I don't know the answers to anything when it comes

to you,' Miranda threw back at him and, gratifyingly, he was the first to look away.

'No wife. No girlfriend. No children lurking in the background.'

'I'm surprised you haven't got hordes of women stampeding you with their attentions.' Why had she said that? She didn't want to go down this personal road of recrimination. She wanted everything to be kept on a purely business level, or else how would she be able to function? But her heart was obviously in disagreement with her head and her bitterness was too close to the surface to allow reason the space to make its own rules and follow them. 'After all, you said it yourself. You're rich, single and eligible. Wasn't that why you were so eager to encourage my assumption that you were a simple caretaker with nothing on his mind but chopping logs and looking after his boss's property?'

'I haven't noticed any hordes of women outside my front door recently.' He didn't appear inclined to enlarge on this simple statement, but she remained stubbornly silent, willing him to continue even though she knew she would recoil from what she heard. It was too easy to picture this man with a woman.

'I finished with my last girlfriend six months ago.' He laughed drily in the face of her incredulous disbelief. 'She wanted marriage, kids, the whole nine yards, and I couldn't promise her that.'

'So you did the kind thing, did you?' Her voice was edged with sarcasm but he didn't rise to the challenge of justifying himself. He wasn't sorry for what he had done, she thought resentfully, he was sorry for *her* and would keep his temper under lock and key, giving her the room to vent her frustrated anger for however long she wanted. She asked tightly, 'What was she like?'

'Tall. Dark-haired.' He shrugged. 'Extremely self-possessed.'

Unlike me, Miranda thought with savage jealousy. 'What did she do?'

'For a living?'

She nodded, determined to go down this road even though it was like walking on broken glass.

'A barrister.'

'Ah. Right. No wonder you thought I was a pathetic, helpless encumbrance.'

'That's not all I thought,' he qualified softly, but Miranda was too consumed by the self-inflicted pain of her own curiosity to hear the indistinct murmur.

'A bruised girl on the lookout for a rich partner to take over from the last one.' She raised fiery eyes to his. 'And what makes you think I won't try to work my feminine wiles on you now that I know what you're worth?'

'What makes you think I…? No.' He shook his head and stood up. 'Your father will be wondering what's happened to us,' he said curtly, moving towards the door and then pausing to wait for her. 'I'll get a contract prepared for signatures by Wednesday, then we can go and see the house. You can get a feel for the place.'

'We?' Her mind leap-frogged to the one snag she had not taken into consideration: the fact that she would be in his presence.

'It *is* my house,' he said wryly, as she walked towards him falteringly. 'And I intend to get very involved in every step of the work. If you think that poses a problem, then I suggest you tell me now.'

'A problem? Why should it pose a problem?' She tilted her head to look at him evenly. 'Like I said, Luke, from here on in what we have is solely a business arrangement.'

CHAPTER SEVEN

THREE weeks later, she could barely remember what had led her to assume that their business arrangement would involve him appearing on her horizon on an occasional basis only.

What she had not expected was to have him around, all day, most days, hovering over her shoulder like a guilty conscience while she liaised with the various builders, instructing them what to do. Whenever she bent her head to inspect some aspect of her designs so that she could discuss them with Tom, the architect, his dark head seemed to be next to hers, examining the same piece of paper, asking questions, discussing, pointing out small improvements or alterations on the original design work. He appeared to have nothing of greater importance on which to focus and it was slowly driving her crazy.

He was the constant thorn in her side, never giving her enough space to distance herself from him. And, consequently, their business arrangement, which she had optimistically assumed would kill off all feeling she had for him, was gradually turning into a battleground of unspoken emotion.

She was now so acutely sensitive to his presence that she could feel him even before he made his appearance in whatever room she happened to be in. And because he never gave her any forewarning as to when he was likely to materialise, she spent her days in nervous expectation of his unannounced arrivals. The fact that he was extremely pleased with her progress was little consolation.

'Haven't you got anywhere else to stand?' she asked irritably one afternoon, as she stood running her eyes over one of the bedrooms, trying to ascertain how it would look completed and what colour furnishings she should advise him to try.

'Sure.' He strolled over to the bay window and then perched on the window sill so that he was now in the middle of her visual scan. As usual, his work jacket had been replaced by a weathered Barbour in a similar deep green shade as her own; and his charcoal-grey tailored trousers were incongruously tucked into a pair of functional though extremely muddy boots.

Whilst alterations to the basic house were not that extensive, the place was still unfit for clothing of a formal nature. The carpets had all been ripped out in preparation for wooden flooring, which he intended to use downstairs, and the bare floors and lack of curtains lent the entire house an air of work in progress.

'You're still in my way.'

'What are you trying to visualise?'

'I'm trying to visualise you going away and letting me get on with my work.'

'I didn't think I was interrupting you...' His eyebrows shot up in innocent amazement and Miranda clicked her tongue impatiently. He was nothing if not deeply respectful of her initial demand that their relationship be kept strictly business. Not once had he mentioned the cabin, or the fraught and life-changing few days they had spent together there. It might not have had existed as far as he was concerned. She had quickly realised that, whilst they may have been fraught and life-changing for her, they were a distant and forgotten memory for him.

'Well, you are,' she snapped, her eyes finally coming

to rest on his formidable body positioned where she could not relegate his presence to the background.

'You're tired,' he suggested mildly and Miranda gave him a dry look.

'I'm tired of you traipsing around behind me.' She sighed, sitting on the ground and resting back against the wall with her eyes closed. She yawned, realising that he was right. She was weary and hungry. 'I mean, Luke, haven't you got an empire to run? I thought you could only spare three weeks out of the year to recover from your stressed existence?' With her eyes shut, she was unaware of him coming towards her until she heard the rustle of his clothes as he sat down beside her.

She felt herself shiver involuntarily and wondered whether he was aware of her reaction to his proximity. She had spent the past few weeks slavishly making sure that she maintained a mask of iron self-control, never letting it slip to reveal the effect his intrusive, disturbing presence had on her. But, while that supported the fiction that he was nothing now but an employer, it also worked against her, allowing their conversations to roam unchecked, allowing his flashes of wit to penetrate her defences and take root in her already treacherous heart.

'My vice president is covering for me,' he murmured, his breath tingling in her ear as he turned to look at her averted profile, nakedly exposed, as it always was now, with her hair ruthlessly scraped away from her face and tightly weaved into a plait that hung down her back like a rope of pale silk. 'And I do keep in close touch with the office. Have laptop, will travel.' They remained in silence for a few moments until Miranda became aware of a more profound silence. The silence of no men working and her eyes flew open.

'Where are the builders?' she asked, edging very

slightly away from him and regretting that she hadn't kept her eyes shut because her vision was now too full of him for her liking. 'Shouldn't they be working?'

'Gone. I let them off early as it's Friday.'

'Gone? But it's only...' She looked at her watch and gasped. 'After six. I have to go!' She stood up, tugging down the Barbour and feverishly sticking her hands in her pockets to make sure that her wallet and car keys were in place. 'I have to get back to London,' she babbled, 'I'm going to be late. I should have left at five.'

'Where are you going?' His tone was expressionless as she flew down the stairs and he followed in her wake, his long legs making it easy for him to keep pace with her.

'Where are my books?' She spotted them on the matting by the window at the bottom of the stairs and snatched them up, struggling under the weight as she fished into her pocket for the car keys and zapped open the car.

'I asked you where you're going.'

'Out,' she said, veering away from the flat insistence in his voice.

'Well, you'll have to cancel.' He trapped her as she leaned against the side of her car, the palms of his hands flat on either side of her.

'What do you mean I'll have to cancel? I made this arrangement a week ago and I have no intention of can-celling! I haven't been out of the house for weeks!'

'Sorry,' he said calmly, without a trace of apology in his voice and he bared his teeth in something approaching a rueful smile but which instead seemed forbiddingly im-placable.

'You have no claim over my leisure time.'

'Nor do I intend to,' he ground out, darkly looming as the cold breeze whipped his hair into a black tousle. 'But

I'm going to be out of the country until next Thursday and Tom wants certain decisions made before I go about placement of the conservatory. I need to discuss it with you.'

'Can't it wait?' Miranda asked, as visions of the theatre with her friends began receding into the distance. Having virtually cut off all ties with a number of her friends, bar a handful of her closer ones, she had made a deliberate effort to try and arrange a get together, if only to prove to herself that she was still capable of having a good time without Luke Decroix around. She also vaguely wanted to prove to her father that her social life had not nose-dived, that she had not suddenly turned into a demented workaholic which he seemed to be smugly encouraging.

'Can't yours?'

'How long will you be?' she asked and he flashed her a smile of triumph, pushing himself back from the bonnet of her midnight blue hatchback.

'Oh, an hour at the most,' he said, stepping back to allow her to climb into her car. 'Why don't you meet me at say...' he flicked back the cuff of his Barbour to look at his watch '...eight? In the Scarpetta brasserie in Hampstead. We can discuss these plans over something to eat.'

Something to eat. A brasserie. It would be the first time they would be together without the reassuring chaperone of builders, the house and, usually, Tom. Miranda felt her heart lurch in protest at the prospect of an intimate dinner for two. She licked her lips nervously and tried to think of some reasonable excuse why that idea could be vetoed. Under the expectant, glittering stare of his blue eyes, in-spiration failed her and she heard herself stutter out an agreement.

One-and-a-half hours later, Miranda glanced to check

her reflection in the mirror in the hall. Working on the house had negated the need for make-up and, when she had opened the drawer to her considerable array of face paints and had begun applying foundation, blusher and the usual assortment of make-up she had always worn, her fingers had worked the colours uncertainly across her face, hesitant through lack of use. It didn't show. The face that looked back at her was radiant. A little *too* radiant, she thought dismally, considering she was supposed to be heading off for a meeting she did not want in a restaurant.

The outfit, which she had considered prim and suitable for the occasion, now seemed provocatively demure; but it was far too late to change; and she sighed at the ribbed deep-rose turtle-neck which she had matched with a casual pair of black jeans and her mid-thigh black coat which flared as she walked.

'Very fetching,' her father said from behind her. 'And what play will you be seeing tonight, my dear?'

'The play's been cancelled,' Miranda said, turning around and bending to retrieve her black and cream checked bag from the ground. 'In fact, plans have changed and there's no theatre tonight.'

'Why not?' Her father gave her an anxious look and she grinned at him.

'Too boring!' she declared wickedly. 'We decided that we'd just catch a plane to Paris and live it up for the weekend.'

The mild anxiety turned into full-blown dismay. She could read his thoughts as easily as a large-print book. He had been as happy as sandman ever since she had begun working and her social life had spiralled down to zero. He must now be wondering whether her zeal for her new-found career was beginning to flag in the face of all those

tempting and pointless activities that she had embraced
with such enthusiasm in the past.

'You didn't!' The two words of horror spoke volumes.
He was positively bristling with disappointment, she
thought, beginning to laugh.

'No, I didn't,' she said, putting him out of his misery.
'Actually, my boss has decided that he needs to see me
to discuss this house of his and he's forced me to cancel
my evening.'

'*Forced* you? I didn't think such a thing was possible.'

'To know him is to understand,' Miranda replied
gloomily. 'The man assumes that he can ride roughshod
over anything and anyone if it happens to suit him. Anyway, Dad, the taxi's going to be here any minute. You
can reach me on my mobile if you need me.'

'Darling, I wouldn't dream of interrupting your evening
with Luke.'

She opened her mouth to tell him that her 'evening with
Luke' had nothing to do with enjoyment and could be
interrupted at any point for any reason whatsoever, however trivial, but was interrupted by the arrival of the taxi,
and she left her father smiling happily in the hall. Much
to her chagrin. He had been unrepentant about his part in
the cabin fiasco, meekly weathering the storm of her accusations until she had run out of steam, and she hoped
that he was not now interpreting her relationship with
Luke as anything other than a business deal. If he was,
she thought, then he was in for a brutal shock when the
job was finished and they went their separate ways.

The brasserie was reassuringly full by the time she
made it there. There was no subdued lighting, or atmo-
spheric background music; and Luke, who was waiting
for her at the table, had brought his briefcase with him
and was inspecting the plans of the house.

With his attention focused somewhere else, Miranda took the opportunity to look at him. He was wearing a cream cashmere jumper and a pair of deep green trousers and, as he perused the papers in front of him, his sensual mouth was compressed with concentration. His clothes, she had noticed, never seemed to conceal his well-honed bulk. If anything, he was one of those men who roused the imagination by sending some sort of subliminal message that underneath all that cotton and cashmere and silk, was a body fashioned for making love. She was still staring blatantly at him when he looked up and caught her wandering gaze, and she felt a tinge of guilty colour invade her cheeks.

'Manage to cancel your plans?' he asked, putting away the papers as she sat opposite him at the small round table.

'If I remember, you didn't give me much choice.'

'Oh, no,' he agreed, as if the thought had just suddenly occurred to him, 'I didn't, did I?' He beckoned to the waiter and ordered a bottle of wine; then he sat back in the chair and looked at her as if, now that the pleasantries, such as they were, were out of the way, he was free to study her; while she, in turn, attempted not to miss a beat.

'You're wearing make-up,' he observed, 'and your hair's out. Do you know, I've become so accustomed to seeing you with your face bare and your hair pulled back, that it's like seeing someone else.'

'I always wear make-up when I go out,' Miranda countered in a muffled voice.

'Mmm. Shame you had to cancel your dinner date.' He watched her in silence as the wine waiter poured a measure of wine for him to taste, filling both glasses when it had been passed acceptable. 'Were you going anywhere exciting?' He took a sip of wine and continued to look at her over the rim of the glass, his disturbing cobalt eyes strangely unreadable.

Miranda briefly toyed with the idea of a lie, but any such thought was stillborn. Luke would never believe her if she said that she was going to Paris for the weekend. In some weird, unspoken way, he seemed to know her. He certainly knew that she was no longer interested in the superficial life she used to lead. He had managed to prise that much out of her during one of his many infernal wanderings through the house, glued to her side, asking just the right number of pertinent questions to allow a few less pertinent ones to slip in. It was to her credit, she thought snidely, that she had managed to glean a fair amount about him as well in the process.

'It would have been exciting for me,' she answered truthfully, 'I'd planned on going to the theatre, actually, to see *Les Misérables*. I know it's been on for centuries, but would you believe I've never got around to seeing it?' She played with the stem of her wineglass before raising it to her lips and taking a few sips.

'I would, actually,' he confessed with a little laugh. 'Theatre times tend to clash with club hours.'

Miranda looked at him in sheepish agreement. 'Well. No matter. I've rearranged it for next Saturday. Anyway, you wanted to discuss the conservatory. I didn't think there was any problem with it.'

'Just making sure that it's absolutely spot on,' Luke murmured, rubbing his thumb across the cool, wet side of the glass before finishing the contents in one swallow. 'After all, this house is not going to be like my apartment.'

'No?' Miranda felt the tell-tale signs of curiosity. 'What's your apartment like? My designer nose is twitching,' she elaborated hastily, just in case he thought that she was angling for an invitation.

'My apartment…is…very uncompromising, very masculine. Maybe masculine isn't quite the right word. Maybe I should say that there are no feminine touches. Everything is functional.'

'I thought you liked that,' Miranda said lightly, pausing to give her order to the waiter. 'You told me,' she reminded him, 'that you didn't like lots of intrusive women around. I assume that meant bringing bunches of flowers in cut-glass vases and little ornaments as presents.'

'I did say that, didn't I?' He seemed to be playing with the memory, turning it over in his head, trying it on for size. 'But now…' he watched as her glass was refilled, '…now, I'm beginning to think that my apartment days are drawing to an end. A man can only survive happily for so long with minimal furniture, minimal kitchen equipment and an exercise machine in the guest room.'

'So you're hankering for the perfect family home,' Miranda said with a tight smile.

'That's a bit strong, but maybe it's time to think about putting down roots and seeing what happens.'

'And is there anyone you have in mind to fill the vacancy?' She could feel a constricting tightness in her stomach, as if a fist was slowly squeezing her intestines. Of course, it was natural for any man to want a family. Perhaps the house had initiated those thought patterns. Perhaps he had bought the house in response to them. What came first, the chicken or the egg? It seemed bitterly ironic to be renovating the house for the man she loved so that he could lay it at the feet of the woman he would eventually want to share his life with.

'Can I pass on that question?' He laughed as if in response to a joke. It was lost on her, and Miranda grimaced in response. She hoped he would interpret the sour baring of teeth as a chummy, unthreatening smile.

'And you intend to have children?' she asked politely, fighting off an inclination to violent nausea. 'The house is certainly ideal for bringing up a family. Lots of space and a large garden.'

'It certainly is ideal, isn't it? I couldn't contemplate raising a family in London. I grew up in the rolling countryside of Warwichshire and I can't imagine what it would be like to have pavements as your playground and parks on a weekend, weather providing.'

Which, over the superb meal, led to a conversation about the relative values of the countryside versus the city. It was an invigorating argument if she could see her way to thinking that it was all theoretical; but she got the distinct impression that there was now a woman in his life and the thought nagged away at the back of her mind until three glasses of very good wine managed to dull it into relatively obedient silence.

It was only when they were finishing their coffee that the reason for their meeting in the first place occurred to her. They had spent not a minute discussing the plans for the conservatory, an oversight he smoothly brushed over by suggesting that they adjourn to his apartment to view the plans at leisure.

'You didn't bring a car, did you?'

Miranda shook her head and started to say, 'but—'

'Good. My driver can take you home when we're through.'

'It's a bit late…'

'My fault,' he said humbly, holding his hands up in surrender. 'But I really do need to discuss this with you before I leave the country, so that you can make sure that Tom knows what he's doing. If you think your father's going to worry if you're not home, then why don't you

call him. I promise you, though, I'll make sure you're
back before the witching hour.'

He gave her a smile of such persuasive charm that
Miranda's protests shrank into low, inaudible grumbles;
and she watched in silence as he called his driver on his
mobile to collect them outside the restaurant.

While she feverishly contemplated this fresh, night-
marish development looming ahead of her, a trial for
her already frazzled self-composure, Luke conducted a
smooth and effortless conversation. He told her about his
views on the stupidity of driving while under the influence
of alcohol, hence the necessity for him to have a personal
driver if he thought he might be over the limit; he told
her about his job, making her laugh weakly as he portrayed himself as a slave to the office, barely having time
to exercise and therefore needing to install an exercise
machine in his guest room.

In response, Miranda huddled into her coat despite the
warmth in the back of the chauffeur-driven Jaguar and
stuttered out an occasional observation when the only
other alternative would be a telling silence.

They couldn't have been in the car for longer than
twenty-five minutes, although it felt like hours. She heard
Luke tell his driver that he would be ready in about an
hour. She slid out of the car in a flurry of panic-driven
nervousness, following him into the expansive marble-
tiled reception area and up three floors to his apartment.

It turned out to be a suite of the kind usually viewed
in magazines. True, he hadn't been lying when he had
said that it was furnished in the most spartan of styles,
but there was an abundance of muted taste in the décor.
The absence of bright colours lent a starkness to the black
leather furniture in the sunken sitting area, as did the util-
itarian nature of the lighting, which appeared to be com-

prised solely of spotlights and burnished-silver standing lights. Only a Persian rug in the centre, a wash of deep warm hues, gave colour to the room.

But she was not allowed to linger very long in fascinated inspection, drinking up all the outer details that filled the mental image she had of the man himself in her head. He led her into the kitchen, which was almost as large as the sitting room and expensively equipped with chrome appliances, including an impressive cappuccino machine on one of the counters.

'I'm an addict of fresh coffee,' he said wryly, following her gaze to the black and silver machine, 'and I'm particularly fond of cappuccino. Something about all that frothy milk always seems wickedly decadent.'

The words 'wickedly decadent' brought a flush to Miranda's cheeks. She could cast her mind back to one or two wickedly decadent things herself and none of them included the consumption of fresh coffee!

He expertly began operating the complicated-looking machine and, after a few minutes, she was handed a cup of steaming coffee with the requisite one-inch layer of froth on top.

Then he laid out Tom's plans on the kitchen table. The kitchen table was black, solid black wood, with clean, uncluttered lines and was ringed with six metal chairs with hessian seat pads. Miranda looked at it sceptically, then she turned her gaze to Luke who had pulled one of the chairs out and had sat down, his large hand cradling the mug of steaming coffee.

'None of this makes any sense,' she said slowly, moving to join him at the table. Any after-effects of the wine had winged their way out of her head the minute they had left the restaurant and her mind was as clear as a bell. Clear, if still tensely wary.

'What doesn't make any sense?' He had divested himself of the cream jumper and had rolled the sleeves of his plain cream shirt to the elbows. Everything about him was so intensely real; but here, in this apartment, she felt as though she had uncovered yet another layer of this complex man. How many layers could one person have? She wondered. Shouldn't *she* be the complex and mysterious one? No wonder his initial opinion of her had been of a shallow airhead. Probably still thought along those lines. Not nearly as deep, complicated and enigmatic as the lawyer types he associated with.

'This is nothing like the cabin, is it?' Miranda said bluntly. 'All this chrome and black everywhere. The furniture in the cabin was so rustic and, well, lived in. *What sort of man are you?*' she added accusingly. He raised his dark eyebrows in amusement.

'You make me sound like a split-personality misfit,' he said, his mouth curving into a smile. 'Do all your clothes look the same? Are all your shoes the same colour? I'm a man who likes a bit of variety. Don't we all?'

'You know what I mean.'

'I know what you mean,' he concurred obediently. 'I guess, the cabin's much more my style. Old and battered. But three years ago I had someone come in to do this apartment out for me when I bought it and she must have figured that I was the kind of guy who liked being in a high-tech environment.' He shrugged. 'It suits me. I just sleep here. If I need to entertain, I tend to go out to do it.'

'Why didn't you complain when she did it? You're under my skin like a tick,' she said, unable to resist the snide sarcasm, 'so how is that you let someone get away with kitting out an apartment you didn't like? I'm surprised you didn't dog her footsteps every inch of the way.'

'We were lovers when I agreed to let her furnish this,' Luke said bluntly. 'We even had vague plans of moving in together but, by the time it was finished, so were we, and I just never got around to doing anything about changing it.'

'Is that why you're so cynical about the opposite sex?' Miranda asked quietly. 'Because someone you loved let you down in the past?'

Luke lowered his eyes. 'Perhaps. I don't like to think I'm vulnerable—what man does? But perhaps I am. Perhaps there's a part of me that still clings to the wreckage of that disastrous relationship, hence my inability to get rid of all this stuff.' He shrugged his broad shoulders fractionally. 'Perhaps, subconsciously, I feel that if I part with all of this, then I shall finally have to say goodbye to the one woman who broke my heart. Who knows, maybe this whole house business is just an empty hope that I can recreate the thing I've lost.'

Miranda felt tears spring to her eyes. She hoped that they were tears of sympathy for this man sitting before her, head lowered, humbly admitting his own frailty. Unfortunately, she suspected that they might well be tears of self-pity and misery. Every word he had said, had sent a dagger straight to her heart and every syllable had twisted the dagger until she felt as though she was bleeding inside.

'I'm sorry,' she whispered. She placed her hand on his wrist, feeling the fine dark hairs against her palm. His warm hand stirred under hers and he clasped her fingers tightly. His other free hand went to his down-bend head, cradling his forehead, forming a shield against her concerned gaze.

'I hope you won't think less of me,' he murmured, not

looking at her, 'because I've succumbed to this show of emotion.'

'I know it's not easy for you to express your feelings,' Miranda said softly. 'But don't be ashamed.'

'Will you comfort me in my hour of need?'

'Will I *what*?'

He peeped through two fingers and she saw that his shoulders were heaving. Heaving but not with the uncontrollable sobbing of a man who could no longer contain a flood of emotion: his shoulders were heaving with laughter. Silent laughter until the silence could no longer be repressed and he collapsed, still clutching her hand.

Miranda yanked her hand out of his grasp and sat back. 'You…*you*…'

'I'm sorry. I couldn't resist.' He could barely form a coherent sentence amidst his splutterings of mirth.

'That's it!' she yelled. 'You fraud! I'm going!'

'Oh, where's your sense of humour?' he asked, sobering up, but only just. 'The last time I got philosophical with you at the cabin, you didn't hesitate to switch me off. I was just responding to your psychobabble.' He grinned unrepentantly at her and Miranda felt her lips begin to twitch in reciprocal humour. She sat back down and assumed a lofty air of indifference to his infantile clowning.

'Very ice-cold maiden,' he told her, still grinning.

'You mean it was all a lie?'

'Not the bit about us being lovers,' Luke admitted. 'I really did go out with Lizzie; and she really did kit this disaster of a flat out for me as a surprise when I was in New York for a fortnight on business; and we really had planned to move in together; but it all fell apart at the seams. We weren't suited for anything more durable than meals out.

'As it happens, we're still friends. She's gone back to America to live, got married six months after we broke up and has a daughter with another kiddie on the way.'

'I never redecorated this place because I could never be bothered. Always too busy, and eventually I guess I just got used to it—the way you do. Your face,' he added for good measure, 'was a picture.'

There was a strange singing in Miranda's ears. She felt light-headed. He had led her up the garden path, something he seemed very good at doing, but this time she was not annoyed, just stupidly ecstatic that the story that he had concocted and which had sent her spirits plummeting had been untrue.

'If you're quite finished with your little joke, perhaps,' she said in a tetchy voice, 'we might get down to business?'

'Business,' he agreed, looking at her and not moving a muscle. Eventually, he shook himself and gathered the various papers together and, for the next half an hour, they inspected the designs of the house, while Miranda busily took notes about measurements and placement of ceiling lights.

When they had finally finished, he handed the papers to her in a plastic file and sat back with his arms folded behind his head.

'You're enjoying this, aren't you?'

Miranda looked back at him, stuck for words. 'You dragged me away from my plans for the evening. How can you ask me whether I'm enjoying this? I mean…yes, it's been a nice enough evening as evenings go… The food at the restaurant was very good… And I suppose as company goes…' she could feel her heart thumping behind her ribcage and her skin felt hot and tight. It was because of the way he was looking at her, as though every pore, every ounce of his concentration was focused on her '…well, yes, you can be an amusing enough companion when you try…' Why kid herself? Just being in his company, for whatever reason, was enough to make her feel as if she was walking on cloud nine. Without him around, her life was flat.

'Actually, I meant that you seemed to be enjoying your work.'

It took a few seconds for her to realise that she had misconstrued his innocuous observation, and then she went bright red as she frantically tried to recall if she had said anything incriminating.

'Yes, of course!' She breathed in deeply and made a great show of checking the time on her watch. 'Yes, it's fun. I mean, I feel as if I'm doing something useful, which is nice.'

'Nice.'

'That's right!' she snapped. 'Now, what time did you say your driver was coming to fetch me?' She stood up and gathered her hair in one hand, scooping it over her shoulder and, after a few lazy minutes of studying her edginess, he stood up, just as there was a ring on the doorbell. The driver! She could have hugged him!

'You know,' he said softly, as she began walking towards the door, 'there's no need to be nervous around me. Haven't I respected your wish that we keep things purely on a business level?'

Miranda could feel his words stroking the back of her neck, lazily feathering her spine and making the hair on her arms stand on end.

'Yes, and just as well, because I wouldn't have taken this job on if you hadn't,' she said, stoking up some healthy aggression and eyeing the lift door with relief. She pinged the button and waited in silence, with her back to him, as the lift finally arrived and the doors slid open.

'Thank you for the meal.' She eventually turned to look at him, with her bag and the papers clutched defensively against her chest.

'Oh, I'll see you down.' Before she could protest, he had stepped into the lift. He swamped the confined area. If she moved two inches she would bump into him, feel his hard bulk against hers. She kept resolutely to one side, determined not to babble herself into embarrassed silence.

'In case you were wondering,' he said conversationally, as the lift finally bumped and the doors opened, 'it's taken a lot of will-power.'

He held the doors so that she could step out.

'Don't you want to know what I'm talking about?'

'No!'

'Coward. Of course you do.' He strolled past the reception desk, nodding briefly at the uniformed porter. 'Well,' he said at the outer glass doors, 'I'll tell you anyway.' He put one finger under her chin and turned her face to his. 'I remember us making love, Miranda, and it's taken a lot to keep my hands off you.'

Miranda sucked in her breath and half closed her eyes. He would kiss her and she wanted him to with a desperation that terrified her. Never mind logic and reason and the absence of love.

'But business is business,' he said to her parted lips, and he kissed her chastely on the forehead. 'Good night.'

CHAPTER EIGHT

So what did that mean? That he wanted her? Wanting had a time limit that love didn't have, she dismissed categorically for the hundredth time. Wanting was fine when that was what both partners in the game agreed to, but when the scales were top heavy, wanting became a liability. That was just the sort of equation that led a woman to feel desperate, and Miranda had never felt desperate in her life before.

She frowned and stared at the samples of tiles in her hand. It should have been peaceful this past week, working in the safe knowledge that Luke was far away in another country, but she missed his intrusive presence. She missed the way her heart lurched whenever her radar picked up the sound of his car pulling up on the drive outside the house, and that keen feeling of light-headed anticipation as she heard his footsteps getting closer. She missed those wayward conversations that always seemed to sneak like a thief into their normal business discussions, and the little asides of wit that made her smile even when she made a great show of looking up to the ceiling in feigned exasperation. She missed the casual brush of his hand against hers and his proximity as he leaned to inspect some detail with her, his breath whispering against her hair.

She felt like a woman who had finally met her match and, having met her match, no longer knew how to control the situation. Worse, the situation was controlling her. In the uneven balance of their relationship, she was the loser;

and the more she fought to maintain her charade of composure, the more she felt herself sinking into a quagmire that was slowly but surely sucking her into its bottomless depths.

He should have been back in the country on Thursday, but he had called to explain that business was keeping him abroad longer than he had anticipated, so that he wouldn't be around until the beginning of the following week.

'But you have to choose what tiles you want for the kitchen,' she had told him accusingly.

'You choose them for me.'

'Me? I can't do that.'

'Why not? I trust your taste.'

Miranda didn't want to choose the tiles on his behalf. She wanted, she realised dismally, to have him stand next to her, discussing what he wanted and firing her soul with the nearness of the forbidden. But here she was, choosing them. The Aga was to be a deep bottle-green and, rather than clutter the background with an array of patterned tiles, she decided on plain hand made green and cream ones to give a clean look. It would go with the terracotta flooring and with the cream units which would be installed when everything else had been completed.

Tomorrow couldn't come quick enough as far as she was concerned. Her planned theatre visit in mixed company would be a welcome distraction from her thoughts which were driving her crazy. A few men might be just what she needed to get her errant mind back on the straight and narrow path.

She would dress to impress, something she had not done now for so long that she could barely remember the time when her choice of clothing was an all-consuming pastime. She would laugh gaily and shimmer with allure.

She would be witty and provocative and flirt madly with the three men Clair and Jesse had arranged as their dates even if the men in question looked like close relatives of the Hunchback of Notre Dame.

She would, she decided grimly, *have fun*. She used to have fun all the time, and she would get back into the habit of it if it killed her.

Consequently, Saturday found her shopping for something new and thrilling to wear, having been kindly patted off on her trip by her father who had murmured something about all work and no play and what it did to Jack.

'I never thought I'd be telling you this, darling, but it's time you got out and had a good time.' He had raised his eyebrows in mild interrogation. 'One or two chaps going along with you and the girls, I take it?'

'Three chaps, three girls. Who knows, Dad, I might find the man of my dreams.' Ha, ha. The current holder of that particular title was thousands of miles away in America, probably having a very good time without her around.

'On the other hand,' her father had replied with unsolicited pragmatism, 'you might find yourself in the company of another Freddie.'

Which, Miranda thought hours later as she dressed for the theatre, was a very likely prospect. At least, though, they all had jobs. Proper jobs and not token occupations carved out of family businesses which paid lip-service to the concept of hard work.

She had bought a calf length clinging black number with a flatteringly wide scooped neck. Her blonde hair looked almost white against the dark backdrop and her height was further accentuated by three-inch heels. She kept her jewellery to a minimum, slipping on only a thick silver bracelet which was minutely carved with dancing figures and a tiny thread-like choker with a deep aquamarine stone that neatly fitted against the hollow of her neck.

She felt like a million pounds and she told herself fiercely that she would act the part, and act it she did, scintillating for her escort as they all enjoyed a drink before the curtain call. Claire had kindly heeded her request that she never laid eyes on another Freddie clone again, and James was physically the opposite. Tall, dark-haired with wire-rimmed spectacles and a consuming interest in computers. He positively glowed with satisfaction as his date lavished her avid interest in every word he said, her blonde hair radiating like a waterfall of shiny cream silk down the length of her back.

The noisy rumble of voices all around her fuelled her need to sparkle; and in a strange, disembodied way she heard herself chattering animatedly to her date, asking him question upon question about the one subject in the world in which she had minimal interest.

This, she thought, as she settled into her seat and welcomed the dark shroud of the theatre, was what it was all about. Never mind moping and longing for a man who didn't love her! Never mind analysing every word he said and dissecting them for hidden meaning! Never mind her skin tingling at every accidental brush and her imagination being fired by the mere thought of him!

'So tell me a bit about yourself,' James said, as soon as the intermission bell had sounded and they had trooped out to the bar to retrieve the drinks they had ordered before curtain call.

'What is there to tell?' Miranda sipped her white wine and fluttered her eyelashes coyly, feeling a fraud for implying that she was little more than a girl without a care in the world.

'Miranda's a born again work horse,' Clair interjected

laughing, which meant that she had to launch into some spiel about her design work.

'And who are you working for at the moment?' James asked, when eventually she had run out of steam and was contemplating hurrying down another glass of wine before the second half. She would not let herself flag at this early point in her fun evening!

'Oh, no one interesting. Luke Decroix. You won't have heard of him.'

'Everybody's heard of him,' James said depressingly. 'He's a pretty big cheese in the city.'

'Oh, really,' Miranda said indifferently. 'He doesn't seem that much of a big cheese to me when he's dithering over what should go where and why. In fact...' she couldn't resist stabbing home her point '...when he's with me he's an incredibly small processed-cheese-spread triangle.'

'Oh, is that right?'

They all turned and Miranda blinked at Luke, who had edged towards their small circle and was looking at her with an amused smile on his darkly handsome face. *What was he doing here? On her wild fun night of forgetfulness?*

'A processed-cheese-spread you were saying?' which made her shut her astounded, half-open mouth.

'What are you doing here? I thought you were in America!'

'Aren't you going to introduce me to your friends? Where have your manners gone?'

'You didn't tell me you were going to be coming to see this play.'

'I didn't realise that I had to let you know my intimate movements from dawn till dusk, actually.'

Her five-strong party was watching this little sketch

with such obvious curiosity that Miranda could positively feel the questions burning in her girlfriends' minds as they tried to tally together the man standing in front of them with the image she had portrayed of an unexciting employer with too much money and the onset of a paunch.

She skirted over the introductions and was about to turn away, pointedly towards James, when Luke signalled to someone behind her.

'This is Eleanor,' he said, broadening the circle to accommodate a tall, dark-haired woman with a handsome, angular face. Not technically beautiful, but with an attraction that came from the suggestion of a powerful intelligence. Her long hair had been pulled back to the nape of her neck and her clothes spoke of practicality rather than frivolity. A complete contrast, Miranda thought with such overwhelming jealousy that she leaned against James to steady herself, to her own slinky black number which outlined every curve of her long slender body and made no concessions to female modesty. Her fun-at-all-costs dress now seemed silly by way of comparison to Eleanor's severely tailored trouser suit.

'Look…' he finished his drink and glanced around his audience '…Eleanor and I were planning on going on to a jazz club after this with the rest of our party. Why don't you lot troop along with us?' His lazy blue eyes, that had somehow managed to eliminate the rest of the group so that they could focus totally on her, sent her already skittering nerves into free fall.

'Actually,' Miranda announced, 'we were all going to head out for something quick to eat after this.'

'But we'd love to change our plans,' Claire interceded quickly. 'Miranda could do with a night out.'

'Good idea,' James murmured to Miranda, slipping his hand around her waist in a proprietorial fashion; which, she guiltily acknowledged, she could hardly object to. 'Give us some more time to get to know one another.'

She was on the verge of quelling any such hasty objective when she glanced sideways to see Luke looking at her, the expression in his cobalt eyes screened by his thick, dark lashes, and she gave a high, tinkling laugh. 'Why not?' she said gaily. 'Might be fun. The last time I went to a jazz club was four years ago with my father. He'd be very impressed if he thought I might be rediscovering his taste in music.'

Luke gave them the name and address of the club and then, as the bell sounded for them to return to the play, he nodded and shoved his hand in his pocket, his other hand moving to usher Eleanor back to their seats.

'Later, then,' he said, just as Miranda linked her arm through James's and tugged him away, gracefully exiting the bar area and wondering whether Luke's eyes were following her. She might not be the world's most ferocious intellectual, she thought darkly, and she might not possess his date's particular brand of appeal, but she had a good body and she derived a childish kick from flaunting it all the way back to their seats.

There was no sign of Luke in the exodus from the theatre forty-five minutes later; and by the time the taxis had been hailed and they had all been deposited outside the jazz club Miranda's edgy enthusiasm was beginning to feel a little worn.

In fairness, she had told James that, lovely though he was, she was not attracted to him.

'And I'm really sorry if I gave you the wrong impression,' she said, holding him back from their crowd so that she could explain herself.

'You're a bit out of my league, anyway,' he responded with a resigned sigh. 'Still, it was good while it lasted.'

He gave her a shrewd, assessing look from behind his glasses. 'In fact, I would say that you're more in Luke Decroix's league. You're the equivalent to a bottle of champagne and I'm more a house wine kind of guy.'

'*His* league? Ha. Bottle of champagne? Only for to-night, I can assure you.'

And the bottle of champagne was beginning to feel re-markably flat, as they walked into the jazz club and her eyes adjusted to the dark interior.

She had had the duration of the taxi ride in which to contemplate Luke, his relationship—whatever that might be—with the woman he had brought to the play, and the temporary appeal of herself. She was, she decided, like a Christmas toy; all fun in bright new packaging; and while it was being unwrapped, it continued to thrill and excite, as maybe it could for a few days or a couple of weeks; but after that it would no longer be a shiny, sparkling, brand new Christmas toy and it would eventually and in-evitably get stuffed to the back of the cupboard to join all the other used toys that no longer thrilled and excited.

Whereas Eleanor, she thought with miserable dejection, was that long-lasting board game that might not look so glamorous when the wrapping came off, but it would never see the back of that damned cupboard.

So big deal if she was no longer prancing around the world in search of enjoyment. So what if she had decided to work and put her frivolous past behind her, to concen-trate on developing the talent she knew she possessed but had always sidelined? It hardly turned her into a board game like Eleanor, did it?

The rush of daring that had made her accept Luke's proposal that they all meet at the club had well and truly fizzled into a need to get back home and go to sleep by the time she spotted his group in the corner of the room.

As she might have expected, he dominated the small party of five. For a start, they were all seated, while he was standing, his restless eyes flicking towards the door then back to his table. Miranda sought out Eleanor and spotted her sandwiched between two men, speaking and gesticulating and obviously expressing a strong opinion on something, judging from her body language. Probably, Miranda thought with a touch of malice, the state of the world, or some such large, consuming issue.

She trailed behind with James, following her friends as they weaved their way amongst the tables, all of which were occupied. On a raised podium, the jazz group were grinding out an evocative slow piece that spoke of sadness, and it struck an unwelcome chord in her.

There was a bustle of shouted introductions, following which several members of both groups went to the dance floor. Amidst the general shuffle of chairs being brought to add to the table, Miranda found herself sitting next to Eleanor with Luke towering behind them. From the brief snatches of overheard conversations, he was quizzing James about what he did, asking questions about where he lived and firing such informed remarks about the world of computers that poor James was forced to adopt a stance of self-defence lest he was steamrollered into silence.

As the sound of their voices washed above her, Miranda tried desperately to cling to the veneer of sparkle that was growing more tarnished with each passing minute. Eleanor, she managed to glean, worked as a tax lawyer but the sound of the music effectively killed any detailed questions. Eventually, Miranda rose to her feet and turned to James with outstretched hand, ignoring Luke who was a good three inches taller than his defenceless victim and who vibrated with restless energy in a way that Miranda thought might well be deliberate.

'Dance, James?' she shouted, barely making herself heard above the wailing sound of the saxophone.

'Okay, but I'm not very good, I warn you! Look out for your feet! You might find that they're not that recognisable after a few dances with me!'

'Aren't you going to ask your date for a dance, Luke?' Miranda's voice was freezingly polite. 'You surely can't leave her sitting on her own while you lurk behind her. The poor thing might get intimidated.'

'Oh, I intend to dance,' he said, bending towards her so that she could hear him. 'When I'm good and ready.'

Miranda swept James onto the dance floor, her body quickly catching the rhythm of the music and swaying in time to the beat, while James looked desperately uncomfortable as he tried to keep up. She deliberately faced away from the table so that she couldn't let herself be tempted into seeing what was happening between Luke and Eleanor. With her back to them, she could pretend that they weren't there at all and that the evening, which she had started out on with such high hopes of having a swinging time and recapturing some of the carefree gaiety of her former days, had not dissolved into stomach-turning tension.

She was in the midst of encouraging a reluctant James to throw caution to the winds and attempt some more complicated manoeuvres when a hand descended on her shoulder and Luke cut in with no attempt at apology, merely applying sufficient pressure on her arm to make her spin around with seeming alacrity, leaving James to head back to the table and embark on a conversation with Eleanor.

'I told you I would dance when I was good and ready,' he murmured into her ear. His arms were wrapped around her, a lover's embrace.

'And what about your girlfriend?' Miranda asked. 'Don't you think it's rude to ignore her so that you can lurch around on a dance floor with your employee?' He wasn't lurching about. Anything but. His movements were as graceful and attuned to the music as hers were and their bodies fitted together with the familiarity of two people who have shared the intimacy of lovemaking. Aware of this and aware of the beady eyes of her girlfriends, Miranda tried to pull back; but as soon as she did, he tightened his grip so that any more attempts to put some space between their bodies might have resulted in an all out scuffle.

'It certainly is the height of rudeness to ignore a girl-friend,' he agreed into her ear, 'but I doubt Eleanor would mind.'

'Oh, I see. You have that kind of relationship, have you? A new-age, liberal, open-ended partnership which means that you can do exactly as you please and she's denied the privilege of objecting?'

'Oh, you're on Eleanor's side now, are you? That surprises me. I think you're jealous...

'You don't know me at all!' Miranda said urgently. 'And why would I be jealous of someone just because she holds down an important job in the city somewhere and dresses in clothes that would look good on a man?'

'Eleanor doesn't look like a man,' Luke said mildly, and she chewed her lip, regretting her jealous outburst. 'In fact, many people think she's a remarkably good-looking woman. It's to her credit that she hasn't allowed the rigours of her job and working in a male-dominated field to smother her femininity.'

'If you're that enamoured with your date,' Miranda shot back tartly, 'then would you mind telling me what you're doing dancing with me?'

'Having an invigorating discussion, I thought.'

'Well, you chose the wrong person. I'm not into invigorating tonight! Try your girlfriend!'

'I hate to say this, Miranda, but I'll put you out of your misery. She's not my girlfriend. In fact, she lives in Chicago and she's over here for four days on business. It's fallen to me to entertain her, something I have no objection whatsoever to doing as I'm very good friends with her husband and godfather to her youngest child. There, you little spitting kitten, feel better now?' He drew back so that he could inspect her face, then slipped his hand through her hair, cupping the back of her neck.

'It doesn't matter to me one way or another.'

'Oh, yes, it does. You're jealous as hell! Just like I am of that computer nerd you brought with you tonight. And don't think that I'm going to let you off the hook. You're gong to stay wrapped up in my arms on this dance floor until you tell me what's going on between the two of you.'

Miranda tried very hard to bristle at the masculine possessiveness in his voice, *possessiveness to which he had no right whatsoever*, but she had a moment of soaring glee.

'Who is he?' Luke demanded. 'Which plank of woodwork did he crawl out from?'

'You know who he is. His name is James, and he hasn't crawled out of a plank of woodwork. He happens to be a computer analyst and very interesting with it.'

'If you happen to like indulging in never-ending conversations about the mysteries of the computer.'

'It's very informative, actually. Did you know that there are some theories circulating that libraries will eventually die out because books will all be accessible on the computer? So...' she smirked with satisfaction, '...you'd bet-

ter hang on to those decrepit detective novels in the cabin.
They might be worth something one day.'

'You can't be interested in a guy like that.' His grip
tightened around her so that she was pulled further into
him, until the scent of his maleness filled her nostrils like
incense and circulated in her head, making her giddy.

'Why not? I happen to like him. A lot.'

'I know you're lying,' Luke whispered into her ear.

'Oh, really?'

'Oh, really.' He repeated her coolly incredulous protest
with frankly assured assertion. 'Do you think you need
something to distract you from your memories of what we
did? Is that it? Why don't we go somewhere a little quieter
so that we can discuss what a big mistake you're making
if that's the case?'

'You can't leave your date on her own!' Miranda pro-
tested, appalled. She glanced around to discover that his
'date' seemed to be perfectly fine and deep in conversation with one of the men from her group.

'I don't think Eleanor will miss me for a short while.'

He had cleverly managed to steer her sideways across
the dance floor; and, as soon as the music dulled, he
draped his arm over her shoulder and led her out of the
dark jazz area into a side room which was comfortably
furnished with cosy chairs. It was evidently used as a
casual lunch area when there was no live music: a relaxing
room with tables strewn with newspapers and a bar area
that was currently shut.

'You seem to know this pl—'

'Shh.' Instead of moving towards the chairs, he pushed
her against the wall. 'I missed you.'

'You wanted to talk,' Miranda said weakly.

'Yes. Talk about why we're fighting the attraction we

feel for one another. Talk about how much you want me and how much I want you.'

There was that word again.

'I don't want you.' She could feel her breasts pushing against the lacy covering of her bra, straining towards his fingers, aching with the anticipation of being caressed. She felt that if he just touched her body, even through the black tight sheath of her dress, she would explode and be swept away on those treacherous wings of longing that would leave her wanting more. More than it was possible for him to give her.

'Oh, yes, you do.' He snaked his fingers through her hair, capturing her face between his hands, his eyes hot and intent. 'You want me to kiss, to take you right here, right now. I know it. *I can smell it.*'

Miranda's eyes closed and she felt the descent of his face towards hers, then the bitter sweet joy of his mouth on hers, hungrily devouring her and her fragile principles, the thrust of his tongue as it squirmed against hers, compelling her to succumb to desire.

And she did. For a while. For that split instant when all her good intentions were suspended in time under the furious assault to her senses. She kissed him back with a hunger that matched his own, not protesting as his hands groped along her thighs, shifting her dress higher, his fingers hooking over the elastic top of her satin suspender belt.

He had meant it! He would take her here and now, hang the possibility of interruption!

This was the definition of *wanting*. It was something that defied all convention and crashed through all obstacles in a greedy need to be sated. She felt it, too. Felt passion rush through her like molten lava, filling every inch of her body.

Her violent push took him by surprise and she used that window of hesitation to wriggle free of his captive grip.

'No!' she said, shaking. She wrapped her arms around her body in an unconscious gesture of defence.

The glazed look in his eyes began to diminish as his brain rapidly deciphered what she was saying. Miranda moved swiftly to one of the chairs and sat down, not knowing whether he would follow and half hoping that he wouldn't.

'No?' He followed her but, instead of sitting down, remained standing over her, looming with the dark intensity of an avenging angel. 'No?' He shook his head, she didn't know whether from disbelief, bemusement or just plain pique at having his plans to seduce her scuppered at the eleventh hour.

No, she amended silently to herself. *Not his plans to seduce her.* Seduction implied having to work at persuasion, having to lure and entice and enthral, and Luke knew that there was no need for him to do any of those things.

'Why not?' he demanded. 'Isn't it a bit late for maidenly outrage? Isn't it a bit like trying to shut the stable door after the horse has bolted?'

'I don't care what it's like,' Miranda told him shakily, plucking her dress between her fingers, her head flung back so that she could look at him.

'This is ridiculous,' he stormed. He slammed his hands onto the back of the chair facing her and bent forwards, his body thrusting towards her. 'A bizarre charade. We made love, Miranda. Do I need to remind you? We made love in every possible way. Don't tell me you're somehow going to pretend that that never existed!'

'I—I've had a chance to think, Luke,' she replied almost inaudibly, so that he had to crane forward to catch what she was saying. 'I've—changed, and making love is no longer part of my plan.'

'So you've decided to become celibate, have you?' His mouth twisted in cynical disbelief.

'I've decided that wanting someone isn't a good enough reason to sleep with them.'

'And what *is* a good enough reason, Miranda?'

'I want a relationship—I want—I don't know what I want…'

'I'm offering you a relationship.'

'You're offering me a good time.'

'Is there a difference?'

Miranda looked at him hopelessly.

'Is this some protracted brand of revenge?' he asked softly. 'Is that it? A way of paying me back for my so-called betrayal? No, it's not, is it? Then what? Are you hoping that I'll ask you to marry me? Is that it?'

The little pulse in her neck began to jump.

'And what if I did? What if I asked you to marry me? Would you suddenly decide that sleeping with me might be permissible after all?'

'No, I wouldn't!' Her blue eyes flashed angrily as she detected the scorn in his voice. Scorn for a gold-digging woman who had suddenly decided to cling to her principles in the hope that they might reap bigger dividends than a temporary bed companion. Wouldn't it be just like him to bypass the little technicality of love and move straight on to exploitation? Hardly surprising, she thought with sudden savagery, considering how familiar he was with that particular method of handling other people!

'No, you wouldn't *what*? Marry me? Or sleep with me? Would you wait until the gold band was on your finger?'

'I wouldn't dream of marrying you, Luke Decroix! What happened between us, well—it happened, and so

what if I'm still—still attracted to you? That doesn't mean
that I'm going to jump into the sack with you. I'm beginning to realise that life is about more than just taking
advantage of passing pleasures. It's about responsibility
and consequences and—and—'

'Self-denial? Why not throw that on the list as well? I
was fine to bed just so long as we were in the middle of
nowhere, but now that you've become a fully functioning
adult with a fully functioning conscience, it's a different
story. Is that it?'

'Yes!' Miranda said defiantly. Let him believe the
worst. Anything other than believing the truth. Because if
he even suspected how far she had fallen in love with
him, he would know that his persistence would guarantee
the result he wanted. And she would be lost. Even more
lost than she already was.

'Fine!' He pushed himself back from the chair and
turned his back on her, his hands bunched into fists.

'I'm sorry,' Miranda said impulsively, realising that she
was sorry. Sorry that she could not give him what he
wanted because she wanted it so badly herself.

He turned round very slowly to face her and only a tell-
tale dark flush belied the illusion of perfect self-control.

'For what?' He laughed dismissively. 'Believe it or not,
I do actually think that it's a woman's prerogative to say
no and to be respected for saying no.'

This wasn't what Miranda wanted to hear. She didn't
want proof of his inherent fairness.

'I'll understand,' she said awkwardly, 'if you don't
want me to finish the project. If you think that things
might be a bit uncomfortable between us.'

'What on earth would make you think that?' He
frowned and then smiled mirthlessly. 'We have a contract,
Miranda, a binding contract and I have no intention of

allowing you to wriggle free of it so that you can escape the inconvenience of seeing me and having to deal with your decision whenever I'm around. Business is business, after all.'

'I just thought…'

'That you had scarred me for life?' His mouth twisted into a mimicry of a smile, one that sent shivers racing down her spine. 'I think I'll live,' he said, 'to fight another day. Or maybe *fight* isn't quite the word I'm searching for…'

She knew what word he was searching for and what he was trying to tell her: that walking away from her would not be a problem. He had tried his hand and had lost, but his loss was a temporary irritation. It confirmed everything she had suspected, and her expression hardened into sour understanding.

'So I shall see you, as usual, on Monday…'

'Oh, yes. Monday, as usual.' His fingers curled around the handle of the door. 'And I'll want a deadline. You'll be wanting to move onto other jobs, I'm sure, and I want to see things wrapped up as quickly as possible. Don't you agree?'

'Absolutely,' Miranda said, with an expression as freezingly distant as his own.

It would be hard, but it could be done.

Little did she suspect as she slumped into the chair once he had left, how hard it would be.

CHAPTER NINE

SHE only began to realise when, on Monday morning, she arrived at the house to see his car parked outside. She had anticipated an hour or two, at least, of relative calm before he made his appearance. Normally, he dropped by. She had never actually arrived to find him fully installed.

Miranda slowly edged her way out of her car and walked quickly towards the front door, her books of fabric and wallpapers clutched like a barricade in her arms. He said he wanted speed and, accordingly, she would make sure that as many of the soft furnishings were chosen in the course of the week as possible. That way, she could begin the process of farming out the orders for curtains and spreads; and, with any luck, she might even be able to arrange with the decorator to start painting and wall-papering the rooms that were already finished.

She heard voices before she entered the house. The distinctive sound of Luke's deep, commanding voice intermingling with Tom's slightly higher far more plummy tones. She took a deep breath, pushed open the door and, for a few seconds, was destabilised by the sight of Luke in his faded jeans and thick black jumper shoved up to the sleeves to reveal the sprinkling of black hairs on his powerful forearms. His arms were folded and his head was thrown back as though she had interrupted him in the middle of delivering a tirade. He handled his workforce with fairness, but woe betide any one who thought they could relax on the job when he was around, because he was not averse to using invective when he thought it would do the trick.

They both turned at precisely the same time as she walked in and Luke said in a clipped voice, making a show of checking his watch as though he didn't know what time it was, 'I thought you might have been here a bit earlier.'

'I had to stop by to get some fabric books.'

'If we'd known you were going to be this late, we wouldn't have...arrived so early...'

'We?'

'Oh, of course...' He did a poor imitation of absent-mindedness and then called out in a voice rich with implied intimacy, 'Helen! The interior designer's here!'

Helen walked briskly out of the kitchen and Miranda's mouth opened in staggered surprise. She only had the wit to snap her teeth back together into a smile when the small curvaceous blonde emerged from the kitchen with a broad smile on her face. She had a heart-shaped face and the sort of unruly fair hair that still managed to maintain a hairstyle without slipping into the category of unkempt.

Miranda dizzily noticed that, whoever or whatever the woman was, she was certainly not dressed for the business of scouting around a house that was still full of rubble and bits of wood. Her emerald-green suit was far too short and figure-hugging and her shoes were of the kind that necessitated lots of rests in between walking.

'Helen...' he slipped his arm cosily around her shoulders and they faced Miranda as a united front '...this is the interior designer.'

'Whose name happens to be Miranda,' Miranda said, stretching out one hand and allowing Tom to relieve her of her weighty tomes.

'This is fabulous, isn't it?' Her slanting green eyes were

lazily speculative and Miranda swallowed down the surge of bile that had risen up her throat. Her immediate impression was of a woman in her early twenties but, on closer inspection, she could see the fine lines fanning around the eyes and mouth that pointed to someone older, perhaps in her mid-thirties.

'Fabulous,' she agreed hollowly.

'I mean, when this great lug told me that he was renovating a house in the middle of nowhere, I had no idea that by *house* he meant *mansion*.'

'Oh, really,' Miranda said, for want of anything else better.

'Helen's fascinated by what you've done,' Luke said, idly playing with a tendril of fair hair. Miranda noticed that his arm, loosely resting on Helen's shoulders, hovered provocatively over the breasts, which were extraordinarily large for someone of beguilingly diminutive proportions. She folded her arms and forced a smile on her face, tilting her head to one side so that she could assume an attitude of interest, instead of revealing her sudden machiavellian desire to murder.

'Perhaps she could trail along behind you while you work? Maybe even give you a helping hand at choosing colours? Or whatever? It's always so much better to have a second opinion on things like furnishings, wouldn't you agree?'

'I work better alone,' Miranda said tightly.

'Oh, but I think the input would be useful. Have another female opinion to go by. And I *am* your employer.' His cobalt eyes were repressively insistent, and she gave him a curt nod in acknowledgement of the trump card he had played. So much for giving in with good grace! His ego had taken a beating and he was going to rub her nose in it.

'Sure.'

Helen's feline green eyes narrowed in satisfied victory and Miranda beamed back. A fairly terrifying beam. The five foot nothing slip of a woman with the curves that would make a centrefold queen envious, made her feel like a towering Amazon. The fact that she was devoid of all make-up and was garbed in a pair of old baggy jeans and an even older baggier jumper didn't help. 'If you follow me, Helen, we'll start with the kitchen, shall we?'

'And I think I'll come along for the ride.' The rogue arm had returned to its original position across Helen's shoulders, and she linked her tiny fingers through his as they followed Miranda into the kitchen.

'Now,' Luke said, 'why don't we all sit down and have a look at what you've brought along for us to see?'

At the end of forty minutes, during which Miranda had been subjected to account for her choice of everything, from floor tiles to wallpaper border, she felt as though she was going mad. She was forced to endure little shows of affection, the casual brushing of his hands on Helen's arm, the overplayed attentiveness to whatever piece of super-fluous advice her new replacement happened to voice, the high-pitched, girlish voice that seemed so at odds with the coolly assessing expression on her face.

When Helen asked where the nearest bathroom was, Miranda almost expected Luke to spring to his feet and escort her there, but he didn't. He sent her on her trip upstairs, following every inch of her voluptuous move-ments across the kitchen and then shaking his head with a little sigh when she was out of the room.

'Don't you think there's something *peach-like* about her?' he asked Miranda, his eyes still lingering at the empty space of the doorway.

'I hadn't noticed.'

'No?' He seemed to be having difficulty in dragging his eyes away from the vacant spot which would soon be filled by the swaying figure of his latest conquest. 'I'm surprised. Helen has never been able to walk into a room without attracting stares from everyone, men and women alike. She's a qualified chartered surveyor, you know. I used to go out with her years ago and, as luck would have it, I happily bumped into her yesterday.'

Miranda snapped shut the book in front of her. And where, she thought acidly, had he managed to bump into her? His little black book perhaps? Let him play his puerile games, she thought venomously.

'She may well be a qualified chartered surveyor, but you can't really intend to paint the kitchen in bright orange. And I don't care what she says about it being good feng shui.' Especially, Miranda thought, when she had made it sound as though not knowing the ins and outs of feng shui indicated some kind of dinosaur attitude towards interior design.

'A charming suggestion, I thought.'

'Charming but hideous. A bright orange kitchen would look vile.'

'According to you.'

'According to anyone with a modicum of good taste.'

'Perhaps. Toss us that colour chart again, would you?' Which he then proceeded to inspect with the thoroughness of a bank manager inspecting an overdue account. 'Maybe it's a little on the vibrant side. Leave it with me for a few days. I'll think it over.'

'I thought you wanted to get this whole thing finished as soon as possible,' Miranda said nastily. 'Mulling things over for days on end isn't going to get the job done quickly.'

'More haste, less speed. Now, shall we have a look at

the bedroom next?' He raised one dark eyebrow expressively and Miranda gave him another of those stiff, practised smiles. She could hear Helen clipping her way back to the kitchen and there was no need to glance around to watch the satisfied gleam on the cheeks. She could very easily imagine it judging from Luke's lingering look at the woman standing behind her out of sight.

'Did I hear the word *bedroom*?' Helen said, and Miranda gritted her teeth together and stood up.

'Oh-h-h, this is gorgeous, Luke!' Helen opened her arms wide in an all-encompassing gesture as soon as they had stepped into the bedroom, from which the two workmen had hurriedly exited, though not before casting appreciative glances at the small blonde.

The wooden flooring was now fully under way and almost laid and it was, Miranda admitted, a gorgeous bedroom. Large and airy, with two massive bay windows that overlooked the sprawling acres of garden. Despite the condition of the house, the garden had been well-maintained and was landscaped with those imaginative touches that spoke of a previous owner whose focus had been primarily on the lawns.

'Where's the bed going to go?' Helen strolled to one of the bay windows and perched on the edge, her eyes flirting with intent on Luke, who was standing and looking around him, his hands stuffed into his pockets, in a lord-of-all-I-survey attitude.

'I thought greens and creams might suit in here,' Miranda interrupted, dumping two of the books on the work table in the middle of the room.

'Hang on. I haven't answered Helen's very pertinent question. Hmm. Now, where should I put that bed of mine…?'

'Just make sure that it isn't with its back to a window,'

Helen said. 'Very bad feng shui. And, personally, I think bedroom feng shui is *very* important.'

'I really had no idea chartered surveyors were so informed when it came to Oriental house design,' Miranda said blandly. 'Is it part of the course these days?'

She flicked to the page she was looking for and pointed to the colour combination she had in mind.

'Hmm. A little dull, darling, don't you think? We want *alive*, we want *dangerous*, we want something a little more *interesting*.' Helen swivelled the book so that it was facing her and flipped through the pages, finally lighting on a colour scheme comprised of reds and blacks at which she proceeded to jab one well-manicured finger. 'Now, Lukey, isn't this more like it? A girl could be persuaded to do all sorts of things in a room with these colours. They're wild, they're passionate, they're…almost demanding abandon, wouldn't you agree? They're literally *red hot.*'

'Lukey?' Miranda couldn't help a little snigger and Luke gave her a quelling look.

'That's my little pet name for him.' She gave him a quick embrace and then slipped her arm around his waist.

'Charming,' Miranda said. 'Though, personally, I've always thought that pet names should be left for pets.' Besides, she could think of quite a few, more appropriate, pet names for Luke Decroix and they all involved dangerous animals with sharp teeth. 'And what does Lukey thing of the *red* option?' She smiled brilliantly in the face of his scowl. 'I certainly agree with Helen that they would lend a certain frisson to any bedroom.'

'I'll take it into consideration,' he muttered.

'Something else being taken into consideration?' Miranda frowned with apparent bewilderment. 'If you tell me what particular reds you want, I can make sure to order the wallpaper today. I believe, Helen, you said you liked…this one?' She pointed to an alarming wallpaper comprised of swirling deep red patterns interlaced with black and gold.

'I *said* I'll think about it.' Luke slammed the book shut and looked at her. 'You might have to carry on without us,' he said abruptly. 'Just choose the colours for the other bedrooms.'

'On my own?' Miranda opened her blue eyes wide. 'But I thought you wanted more female input? I think it's a splendid idea if Helen shared her thoughts on the décor.'

'I've got to get back to London for a meeting this afternoon.'

'Well, then, why doesn't Helen stay and give me a hand? I'm dying to hear what other innovative ideas she has in mind.' Miranda allowed herself the sheer pleasure of seeing him wallow in the consequences of his own ill-considered plot to humiliate her but her enjoyment was short-lived.

'She can't. She's coming down to London with me…' His blue eyes sent a very distinct message which had Helen gurgling with anticipation.

'But what about your meeting?' she asked coyly, snuggling against him.

'Some things can wait.' As he said that, his eyes flicked to where Miranda was standing awkwardly in the centre of the room. 'So you just get along without us and let me have your decisions by tomorrow lunch-time. Think you can manage?'

'Perfectly.'

'Good. Then we'll leave you to it.' At the door, he paused, his arms still around the small blonde. 'Actually,' he said in a thoughtful voice, 'I have an idea… Why wait until tomorrow when, as you say, I want this whole thing wrapped up as soon as possible...? Helen and I are going to be dining at my club this evening... Why don't you join us for a pre-dinner drink and you can bring samples of what you think I might like. That way, I can make my decision and you can begin sorting it all out in the morning, first thing...'

'I'm busy this evening.'

'In that case, you'll just have to cancel, won't you?' He gave her the address of his club, as though her social life was something that barely qualified to be a minor detail, never mind a reason for refusing his order. 'Be there for seven, would you? That way, we should have the whole thing sorted out and wrapped up by eight-thirty and you can do whatever you had planned...'

Instead of going, he resisted Helen's eager tugs and continued staring at Miranda, waiting for her to speak. It crossed her mind that perhaps he was waiting for more than mere agreement with his high-handed redistribution of her free time. Was he waiting for her to tell him what plans she had? Even though he had no right, was he still jealous that she might be seeing someone? The thought made her fizz with resentment.

An evil little spark sizzled inside her and she lowered her eyes. 'That sounds fine,' she said. 'And I'm sure James won't mind if I meet him a little later.' She risked glancing up at him and, for the merest of seconds, their eyes tangled, but his expression remained unrevealing. What was revealing was the kiss he gave the woman nestled against him. A long, lingering kiss that was more like a taste of the red puckered mouth than a friendly brush of lips against lips.

'See you later,' he murmured, as a red flush crept treacherously along her neck and flooded her face. He smiled and she felt a rush of resentment that was so overpowering that she was tempted to heave the wallpaper book at his dark handsome head.

But she didn't. She spent the rest of the day simmering instead. If he had wanted to prove to her just how little she had meant to him, then he had succeeded; because even if the big-breasted Helen was not the love of his life, she certainly was the embodiment of the transience of his lust. It had been perfectly clear from the body language, not to mention that kiss by the bedroom door which had left precious little to the imagination, that they were bed partners.

The thought of that was so abjectly painful that she tried to shove it away, but throughout the day it hovered there, like a malign imp taking delight in torturing her.

In anticipation of what Helen might be wearing, and she was certain that it would involve a sufficient lack of fabric to enhance her prominent breasts, Miranda went down the road of the opposite extreme. Nothing stretchy, nothing that emphasised her body, nothing that revealed the length of her legs. Instead, she chose to wear a plain grey trouser suit twinned with a light blue cashmere jumper and some flat black shoes.

In deference to the unusually sober attire, she combed her hair back into one long French plait, on either side of which she placed a tortoiseshell hair grip.

When she inspected her reflection in the mirror, she decided that this was an outfit in which she could cope. She felt efficient and professional in it. A woman immune to the attractions of the opposite sex, and of one man in particular. A woman who was the archetypal working woman and therefore would not succumb to feelings of raging jealousy.

She could safely ignore Helen in an outfit like this and if Luke really got on her nerves, she thought with a little nervous giggle, she could always hit him with the robust black leather bag she intended on using.

But when she finally arrived at the club at a little after seven and was shown into the cavernous sitting area around which were strewn small tables, comfortable chairs and faded Persian rugs, it was to find that Helen had not yet arrived.

'There's no need for anyone else to get involved at this stage of the proceedings,' Luke drawled, summoning a waiter apparently from thin air and ordering a bottle of white wine.

'Oh? But what about the importance of additional female input?' Miranda sat back in the chair and crossed her legs. With her samples in her thick folders on the ground and in this austere suit, she could almost maintain the illusion of their boss, employee relationship.

'Perhaps I overestimated that,' he muttered under his breath.

'Well,' Miranda leaned over and collected her folders, opening out the top one on the table in front of them '…shall we get on with choosing these colours?'

'I'll have a look at them when I'm ready.' The waiter materialised, again seemingly from thin air, and poured them both a glass of wine. 'And I'm not ready yet.'

'Well, shouldn't we get this done with before Helen arrives? You might find that she's not happy with the selection and doesn't like the idea of being sidelined.'

'She won't be arriving.'

'Oh.' The single monosyllable spoke volumes and Luke's eyebrows met in a frown.

'That's right. *Oh.*'

'What happened?' She felt a satisfying, sweet singing in her ears and had to force herself to remember that one woman's disappearance from his life meant nothing. It certainly didn't suddenly transform him into a man who was ready to take commitment by the horns, least of all commitment to her. He would just move onto Helen Mark two.

'I decided that anyone who seriously considers decorating a bedroom in deep reds wouldn't be the kind of girl I'm interested in.'

'But you two made such a perfect match!' Miranda sipped her wine and glanced around her idly. 'And she seemed so *enraptured* with you. What a let-down for the poor woman!'

'She *was* a bit disappointed,' he admitted, 'but I managed to paint such a black picture of myself that, by the time she left, I could hear her thinking that perhaps it was for the best.'

'What did you tell her?'

'That I was a serial womaniser with a penchant for train-spotting.' He drained his glass and looked at her over the rim, his black-fringed eyes unreadable. Then he poured himself another, tilting the bottle at her and leaning forward to top up her drink, but she shook her head.

'Anyway, there you go. As they say about the sea and fish...' He stretched his long legs out in front of him and watched her. Miranda was not going to let herself respond to the taunting challenge in his voice.

'I haven't got all evening,' she said politely. 'So if you wouldn't mind...?'

His jaw hardened fractionally. 'Sure. As a matter of fact...' he consulted his watch '...nor have I. Shall we get on with it?'

They spent the next half an hour looking at the various samples she had brought with her, but his mind was elsewhere. She could sense it. He agreed with everything she showed him and it slowly dawned on her that his agreement had more to do with his urgency to get the house finished and her out of the way, than with any inherent good taste she might have displayed.

'So I'll go ahead and order all of these, shall I?' she asked a little uncertainly and he shrugged, not bothering to glance in her direction.

He was looking at the door. Involuntarily, Miranda followed his gaze and felt numb when a tall, dark-haired woman appeared, looking around her before recognising him and waving.

'Candice,' he said in a low voice. 'I thought you might have finished a bit sooner, but…'

'Candice?'

He shrugged helplessly and gave her a charming smile. 'Would you like to stay and meet her? I think you two would get along, actually. She's into houses…'

'She's an interior designer?'

'No, no. Buy and sells properties. Useful contact for you to make, in point of fact.' He was getting to his feet and Miranda hurriedly and dazedly followed suit. Before her brain could catch up with reality, she found herself shaking hands and muttering something polite, while Candice exclaimed over her job, gushingly informing her that they were always on the lookout for new designers.

'And you must be good if Luke trusts you to overhaul his house.'

'Miranda hadn't worked for a while. I was merely lending her a helping hand.' He smiled in a self-effacing manner and Miranda choked back her inarticulate furious muttering.

'Oh, and what were you doing before?' Dark eyes narrowed on her. 'You're much too young to have been bringing up a family…'

'Oh, Miranda was just…'

'Travelling. Anyway, I must dash.'

Trust the rotten swine to start exclaiming about the night being young; and why not stay at least to finish the bottle of wine; surely she and Candice would have so much to chat about. Miranda could quite easily have killed him on the spot. But instead, she threw him a killing smile and gathered her folders together.

'No, as I said, I've got another appointment tonight.' She extended her hand politely to the other woman. 'Have fun.'

She didn't glance back once as she walked the five-mile plank, or so it seemed, from table to door, nodding curtly at the porter as he tipped his hat at her.

If only James had been around, she thought viciously, as the evening air clipped her cheeks and made her sprint to hail a taxi back to the house, he might have been in luck. She might not have been so pre-emptive in being a good girl and telling him that she wasn't interested. She might have played the Devil at his own game.

Of course, she thought wearily, she wouldn't have. Why bother to kid herself? Luke was too big a part of her soul for her to try and discard him in a series of pointless affairs. Or even one pointless affair.

She awoke the next morning with the dull, heavy feeling of not having slept very well.

Now that most of the structural work was under way and the various colour schemes and designs had been chosen, her presence at the house would, of necessity, be less intense. She might be able to go along perhaps every other day, just to supervise that her various touches were being adhered to. Likewise, there was no need for Luke to appear with such regularity. She wasn't surprised when she got to the house, to find that he hadn't made an appearance.

Miranda trailed through the rooms, her mind not focused on the job at hand, but rather on the spectre of Luke in the arms of other women. And, for the looks of things, a line of women without much discernible gap between them. If he intended to use distraction as a means of getting over her, then he was certainly entering into the spirit of easy oblivion with boundless energy.

On the spur of the moment, she found herself ringing James and arranging to see him that evening.

'Perhaps we could go out for a meal,' she suggested desperately, 'and then maybe come back to the house for coffee. Dad has gone away for the next few days. And I...' she drew in her breath and vacantly let her gaze wander around the rolling countryside that spread like a thousand-hued blanket around the house, dwarfing her as she stood by her car, mobile in hand '...I need to talk to someone. Someone impartial...'

'Ah. Just friends, I take it?'

'Just friends.'

'Good. Because you're far too short and plain for me. Okay. What say I pick you up about seven and we go somewhere for a quick meal, then back to your house for coffee and confidences? You can tell me all about him.'

'About who?'

'The man who broke your heart.' He laughed down the end of the line. 'I have three sisters, Miranda, and I've eavesdropped enough conversations as a lad to know that when women say they want to talk, it's usually because someone's broken their heart.'

If only, she thought as, later, she sat in a noisy Italian restaurant with James. If only Cupid went around choosing his victims with a little more discernment, because James was a good listener, and if she were just a little different, then maybe she could have fallen for him and thereby spared herself the promise of lifetime's misery.

As it was, she spent the better part of an hour pouring her heart out, with intermittent breaks during which she apologised profusely and promised not to be such a relentlessly boring female the next time they met.

'He's just trying to make you jealous,' James said, as she lingered over yet another detailed description of replacement number two, and Miranda snorted.

'Of course he's trying to make me jealous. He wants to make sure that I realise how much I want him and absolve himself of all blame. He wants to prove that however much he wanted me, it wasn't enough to make him pine when I turned him down.'

It was nearly nine by the time they returned to the house and she felt pleasantly tipsy and marginally better than when she had set out two hours earlier.

As she let them in through the front door, she held his hand, guiding him towards the sitting room and giggling as she groped along the side of the wall for the light.

'My father is obsessed with switching lights off,' she whispered, still feeling the wall for the switch, her body turned towards James and her face tilted as she giggled merrily. 'I've told him a million times that it makes no sense to pretend to save money on electricity, then have a tumble drier, but he's never seen the logic of my argument. You do, though, James, don't you?'

She realised that she was asking more than an answer to that simple question. She was asking him to justify the decision she had taken to walk away from Luke when an insidious voice in her head kept telling her that maybe she should just have taken what was on offer and run. If she was going to suffer, then why not have something to show for it at the end of the day, instead of a halo that felt too heavy for her head and a lot of pious self-pity that made the worst bed companion. Wasn't it better to be hung for a sheep than a lamb? Or something like that? Her brain, after three glasses of very average wine, felt a little fuddled.

She was still leaning into James when her finger found the switch and the sitting room was flooded in a soft mellow light that swam over the centre of the large room, leaving the corners in semi-darkness.

'Honestly, James,' Miranda said huskily, with a sob at the back of her throat, 'it's been so good being with you. I'm really glad we got together. Shall we have a coffee? And carry on if you're not too tired with the whole thing?'

She tugged him by his wayward tie into the room and only became aware that something was wrong by the expression that registered on his face as he looked beyond her. The smile froze on his lips and he said, in a low, singsong voice,

'Uh-oh.'

Miranda turned around very slowly, and Luke's voice reached her ears before her blurry eyes could discern him sitting on a chair towards the back of the room.

'You were saying, Miranda? About carrying on? Please, don't let me stop you in mid-sentence.' There was dangerously reined control to his words that made her nervously turn to James for support. James however did not look like a man who was about to rush into the arms of danger in his continuing role of moral supporter.

'Perhaps I'd better go,' he said slowly.

'No!' Miranda screeched. She hesitantly took two steps into the sitting room, arms folded warrior-style. Then, remembering that it was, after all *her* house, or at least her father's, she boldly took two more steps before stopping well short of her target.

'What are you doing here?' she demanded.

'Hadn't we better dispatch your escort before we launch into conversation?' He lazily clasped his hands behind his head and tore his eyes away from Miranda long enough to say to James, 'Run along, little boy.'

'There's nothing,' Miranda said, with a lot more courage than she felt, 'that you can say to me that you can't say in front of James.'

'I beg to differ. Now, boy, are you going to go of your own accord or do I have to throw you out? Because, make no mistake, I'm more than capable of dispatching you into the street. Head first.' Unconsciously, or perhaps as an unspoken threat, he slowly flexed his fingers.

A successful ploy as it happened because she heard James say nervously from behind her, 'Will you be all right, Miranda?'

'She'll be absolutely fine.'

'Don't believe a word of what he says!' she exclaimed in a frantic outburst. 'I've told you that he's a congenital liar!'

'So you've been talking about me, have you?' Luke stood up and moved with purposeful slowness towards them.

With a little sign of frustrated resignation, she turned to James and said, 'It's all right. You'd better go.'

'Wise advice.' Luke was now only a couple of feet away from her and up close, with the light more directly positioned over him, she could see the smouldering fury stamped on his dark features. 'I'll give you ten seconds; then, my friend, I want to hear that front door slam behind you.'

CHAPTER TEN

'SOUNDS like he's gone.' Luke lazily relaxed into his chair with a triumphant smile. 'So much for your rescuer. He couldn't wait to run away when the going got a bit tough. You're going to have to do a bit better than that, you know. There's nothing worse for a budding relationship than for the man to feel that his woman is the aggressor. Call me old-fashioned but I happen to think that the healthiest relationships are the ones where the man can consider himself the protector. Now, why don't you sit down?'

'Call me old-fashioned, but I happen to think that breaking and entering is an offence. And I am *not going to sit down*!'

'You sounded a little worse for wear when you came in. Haven't been out drinking, have you? Weak men find it very easy to take advantage of a woman when she's drunk.'

'I am not drunk!'

'No? Well your face looks a little flushed considering you're not drunk.'

'I'm flushed with outrage! *What* are you doing here and how did you get in?' Miranda continued to skewer him with furious blue eyes, her hands placed firmly on her hips.

'Sit down.'

'I will *not sit down*! And stop giving me orders in my own house! How dare you? I don't know how you found your way inside here but...'

'How do you think I got in? Broke a window-pane and crept in? De-alarming the house in the process?'

'Well, how did you?'

'I won't be answering any more questions until you sit down. And I won't be leaving either.'

Miranda flung herself into a chair and her short skirt rode up her thighs, exposing a slither of bare skin where her stockings ended and her suspender belt began. She barely noticed Luke's narrowed eyes as he absorbed the pale strip of flesh, nor did she hear the softly indrawn hiss.

'I came in through the front door,' Luke told her shortly. 'And I switched off the alarm using the code your father very kindly gave me.'

'My father...'

'Knows that I'm here. Why are you dressed like that?'

Thrown off course, Miranda could only stammer out a reply. 'Dressed like what?'

'Like a cheap street walker.'

'Like a...*how dare you*?' She unconsciously held her hand to her throat, pulling together the front break in her tight, fitted woollen top. She could feel the little pulse in her neck throbbing against the backs of her fingers.

'Did you go out tonight with the thought of provoking a response? Is that why you're dressed in a skirt that barely covers your underwear?' His voice was controlled but she could detect a dangerous edge to it that spoke of emotions barely reined in.

'This skirt is perfectly all right!' Miranda snapped, distracted once again from the more perplexing mystery of what he was doing in her father's house. Nevertheless, her fingers fluttered guiltily towards the hemline, vaguely aware that because of the way she was sitting, there was more skin exposed that she cared for.

'I hope you weren't stupid enough to let that little boy touch you...'

'Little boy? James is hardly what I would call a little boy!' She was referring to his height, but she could tell from the sudden darkening in his eyes that his mind had taken her innocent sentence and reworked it into something more sinister. She watched as he clenched his powerful fists, and she felt a stirring of satisfaction.

'And what would you do if I *had* let him touch me, Luke?' she taunted. 'There wouldn't be much you could do about it, would there?' She sat back, allowing her hands to drop to either side of her because there was no reason for her to feel guilty or to be propelled into defending herself against someone who had no right to be there anyway.

'I wouldn't bet on it.' His voice was a low growl, like the rumble of thunder and, before she had time to react, he had moved swiftly to the sofa where she was sitting. 'You don't want to find out what I could do,' he said, positioning his bulky body so close to her that she had to cringe back to avoid physical contact. Along the back of the sofa, his extended arm found her silky hair and curled into it so that she was imprisoned. 'Don't mistake me for one of your mild-mannered businessmen who's scared of a little physical—shall we say—retribution...or for one of your craven playboys who wouldn't know a street fight if it hit them in their pretty little face.'

'Oh, very tough,' Miranda mocked. She kept her head rigidly still, but even so she could still feel the weight of his hand in her hair. The low front slit of her jumper had made wearing a bra pointless and she was uncomfortably aware of her breasts pushing against the fine woollen fabric. Thank heavens only the shape of her breasts was contoured by the wool, which was not thin enough to reveal the circles of her nipples.

'And why does it matter anyway?' she asked in a trembling voice. 'We're not involved with one another, Luke. Or is it all right for you to prance about testing all the fish in the sea, while I sit at home chewing my fingernails and...' think about you, she thought '...watching television... I don't need you checking up on my movements! I'm a free agent and I can do exactly as I please. With *whoever* I want!'

'I haven't been testing all the fish in the sea,' he muttered, flushing, and there was a profound silence that lasted the duration of a heartbeat.

'Oh, and what about Helen, the-woman-who-turns-heads wherever-she-goes-she's-a-chartered-surveyor-you-know? And Candice, the great, important property developer who could help me out because she has so many contacts?'

'Distractions.'

The single word was like a match set to dry leaves and Miranda did something she had never done in her life before: she swung at him. As the soft flesh of her palm made contact with his cheek, she watched in horror as his face swivelled under the impact. His hard jaw line reddened immediately with the imprint of her hand and he nursed it while he watched her with dry amusement.

'I—I'm sorry,' she stammered. 'I—does it hurt? I'll get a wet rag...' She half stood up and he pulled her back down with his free hand, which he left loosely circling her wrist as she tried to fix herself into a less revealing position.

'Don't. I deserved that.'

'You *deserved it*?'

'For being a fool.'

Miranda looked at him, her lips parted. He gave her a rueful glance. 'You pack a hefty punch. I don't suppose you've ever considered taking up boxing as a hobby?'

'I've never hit anyone in my life before,' she said in a stunned voice.

'I consider myself lucky to be the first,' he mused. 'You once told me that you weren't a jealous kind of woman. But jealousy is a very telling emotion, don't you think? I personally think that it's one of the most primitive of human feelings. It can rise out of nothing, and when it takes over, it can command our entire body, make us do its bidding. I shouldn't have used that word. *Distractions.* But that's what Helen and Candice were. Distractions and manifestly unsuccessful ones at that.'

'What do you mean?'

'I mean that I haven't slept with either of them, nor did I want to, despite their obvious physical attributes.'

Miranda felt a tide of relief and joy rush through her.

'I thought…' he began, pausing and searching, apparently for the right words. '…I thought that I would be able to forget…forget you…but it appears not. And you can't forget me either, can you?' He gave a dry laugh. 'I saw it on your face when you met Helen at the house and, I tell you what, just witnessing that expression was enough to have made it worthwhile because I wanted you to be jealous. I wanted you to be eaten with jealousy so that you could realise how much you wanted me and how much you didn't want to share me with anyone else. I wanted you to feel the same way about me as I do about you.'

There he went again, Miranda thought with a little sigh of misery, *want, want, want.* But his still, words were like soothing unguents to her troubled mind. She had fought her love and their intense attraction to one another with the only weapon she'd had at hand; her morality. But it had not been enough. It hadn't even been enough to blunt the intensity of her feelings for him.

He took one of her hands between his and traced the lines of her thin fingers, his head lowered in apparent concentration.

'I wasn't prepared for this,' he murmured inaudibly. 'When you descended on me in that cabin, my first thought was to get rid of you as soon as I could. I figured that I'd met enough girls of your ilk in my life to be able to spot an empty-headed pretty face from ten miles away.'

'I know. You said as much.' Miranda followed the line of his fingers with her eyes, sadly wistful because she could feel her capitulation and what it meant.

'I did, didn't I?' He glanced up at her sombre face and smiled, willing her to smile back at him. 'Then I realised that I knew who you were. Had heard your father talk about you. He's very proud of you, you know, even though you haven't exactly used your talents to their advantage, at least not until now.'

'Oh, thanks very much. Nothing like cutting to the quick.'

'It's the truth.' Luke paused. 'In a way, it seemed as though fate had thrown you in my way and the thought of that amused me. You see, your father had even tentatively hinted once that you and I might be...what shall I say...suitable for one another? At the time, I laughed outright at any such suggestion; but when you arrived, well, you know what happened. If you had been anyone else, I wouldn't have dreamt of concocting any plan to bring you in line.

'But I realised almost immediately that my preconceptions of you were wrong, that you were more complex than I had bargained for, and when your father jokingly suggested that I might be a good influence on you I found myself jumping at the idea. I told myself that it was the challenge, but there was something else. Something I couldn't quite put my finger on, and I've never experienced anything like that before with a woman.'

'I had no idea you knew my father that well.'

'Professionally, mostly. But we did have dinner together now and again, just to cement the bond he had with my own father.' He sighed and looked at her. 'Is this making any sense to you? I'm trying not to sound confused, which is how you make me feel.'

'Oh, what's there to be confused about?' Miranda sighed and stood up, pulling her hand out of his reach and hugging herself as she strolled towards the window and parted the thick curtains a crack to stare outside. Then she let the drapes fall back into place although she remained where she was, leaning against the window sill, which made a soft perch with the heavy fall of velvet cloth.

'I landed on you and practically forced you into sleeping with me.' Miranda looked at him steadily. She was aware that the evocative fluency of his words could start a whole network of hope burgeoning inside her and she wouldn't let that happen. She would be realistic, if nothing else, because what he was speaking of had nothing to do with love.

'Oh, is that what you did? And I thought I might have had some say in the matter.' Luke had angled his big body so that he was facing her but, even with the distance she had put between them, she could still feel the potent effect of his personality curling around her like a suffocating vice.

'What man wouldn't say yes to a woman who throws herself at him?' Miranda asked with a tight laugh.

'This one, actually.'

'Maybe.' She shrugged, determined to summarise the so-called course of their so-called relationship. Because putting it into words would leave no room for the romantic notions festering unbidden inside her. 'So now you tell me that I confuse you. Why? Because you hadn't expected that you might want a one-night stand to proceed into an affair?' Her fingers fiddled restlessly with the woollen top.

'I suppose I should be flattered, should I? Or maybe, it would have died a natural death if I hadn't been an interior designer and you hadn't had a house to design. Maybe then you wouldn't have had an excuse to find me work to do to save me from myself; and then you wouldn't have been thrown into my company so that you found yourself remembering a few hours of lovemaking a million years ago, wanting to turn those hours into a few days or weeks, or however long it takes before a man like you gets bored and needs to stretch his wings and move on.'

She couldn't bear to meet his eyes, so she stared behind him to the doorway. 'And you knew you'd win, didn't you? All you had to do was be patient and, in the end, I'd break down because you could read it on my face. You told me so yourself.'

'Oh, for God's sake, Miranda.' He raked his fingers through his hair and stared at her with frustration. 'Why are you making this sound all so damned sordid?'

'It's all about having a fling, Luke. I'm not making anything sound sordid. I'm just being practical.'

'Well, stop being so bloody practical. You have no idea what I've gone through...'

'Oh, I can well imagine. Sleepless nights wondering how to get me back into bed! Tortured hours thinking of ways to change my mind!'

'Stop it!'

'Why?' Miranda knew that she was going wildly off course now, thrashing about in waters that made her want to break down in front of him, but she couldn't seem to help herself. 'I know what you want so why beat about the bush with fancy talk about feeling confused and confessions of what you felt and when you felt it? Why not just call a spade a spade and we can get down to business. Because you're right. The attraction hasn't stopped for me either.' She reached and pulled her small top over her head, flinging it carelessly on one of the chairs.

'Miranda, don't!' His sharp voice was like the crack of a whip, and she paused with her hands already poised to leap on him. She could feel the hot, blinding force of her tears hovering just behind her eyelids, but she would not cry. Wanting him and sleeping with him was a poor man's substitute for the love she desperately craved, but it would have to be enough; because those few weeks of being in his presence had made her realise that fine principles were one thing, but reality was another.

'Don't,' he said in a more gentle voice. He stood up and walked over to where she had dropped her arms to her sides and he rubbed them with the palms of his hands.

'Why not?' she asked in a small, resigned voice. 'It's what you want, isn't it? It's what we both want.'

'But not like this.'

He slipped one finger under her chin and tilted her head so that she was looking at him. 'I would rather die than ever be the one to make you cry,' he whispered, wrapped his arms around her, and drew her into his great bulk. She could feel the thudding of his heart. It was unbearably comforting.

'I'm not crying,' she said stubbornly, and she felt him smile.

'But you want to, my darling, and it's my fault. I was blind.'

'Don't speak,' Miranda said softly. Sometimes words could be knives and she just wanted to stay where she was, in the cocoon of his arms, kidding herself that everything was going to be all right.

'Don't be afraid,' he whispered into her ear. 'I never meant to hurt you. I just didn't realise that you would get to me the way you did and it frightened me. I've always had my life under control and it was a new experience for me to find myself caught up in an undertow without any idea where it was leading. I would have followed you, you know. Whatever. Yes, it was handy that I had an available excuse but, if I hadn't, I would have just thought of one because, the day you left that cabin, I knew that I couldn't live without you in my life.'

Miranda felt her shuddering body go very still at that.

'I spent those days after you left telling myself that I was a fool, that sleeping with you, however magical it had been, was not essentially different than sleeping with any woman, but I was wrong. I came back over here with your designs, like an idiot on a quest to prove the impossible. I desperately wanted you back in bed with me and I was infuriated that you were so adamant that you would design my house but nothing else would be on the agenda. You can't begin to imagine what I felt when I saw you with that little twerp. It was as though my entire universe had come crashing down on my head. I never want to go through that again, my love.'

He rocked her gently, drawing comfort from having her in his arms. 'Even when you told me that you wouldn't entertain the idea of sleeping with me, I still imagined that you hadn't dealt me a mortal blow, that I could deal with that the way I had dealt with everything else in my life. With efficiency. But I was wrong and I was blind. I need you, Miranda and I've never said that to anyone in my life before. I need you and I want you and I love you.'

'You *what*?'

'I love you.' He drew back so that he could look down at her and gave her a crooked, stupified smile. 'And it just took me time to realise how much that one thing could change the whole equation…'

EPILOGUE

MIRANDA stepped into the room and felt Luke step in behind her, enfolding her in his arms, his hand wrapped possessively around her heavy breast.

It was a small room, with two quaintly shaped semi-circular windows overlooking the gardens, adjoining their own bedroom with an interconnecting door. The intention had been for it to be an upstairs study, to be used if Luke occasionally needed to work at night and didn't want to use the massive and well-equipped den on the ground floor.

Right now, the last rays of the summer sun were dipping through the windows, sending a soft, mellow glow through the room.

'I really liked this wallpaper.' Miranda sighed.

'We could always leave it as it is.' He nuzzled her ear and she squirmed pleasurably against him, feeling her soft body relax deeper into his.

'You know we can't. It's too…*blue* and too masculine.'

'And what do you suggest, my little interior designer?' He slipped his big hand under her jumper and felt the heavy weight of her breast and the taut protuberance of her nipple against his palm. He rolled his hand gently around and Miranda gave a little gasp of pleasure. She could feel his arousal pressing against the back of her and she smiled dreamily before refocusing her mind on the task at hand. But she didn't remove his massaging hand. That felt altogether too good.

'How about something orange…?'

'A little vibrant, wouldn't you say?' They shared a laugh of mutual understanding at this private joke.

'But very good feng shui. And also very neutral. Besides, bright colours suit little children…' She gazed at the room and saw oranges and yellows and turquoises and a small wardrobe with a montage of ducks swimming across the doors and, just there, the cot. She saw a little baby lying in it, with fuzzy dark hair, growing into a toddler, and the hurried, frantic patter of tiny feet racing through a house. She placed her hands on her stomach, already swelling and showing the five months of pregnancy, and Luke's hands covered hers.

Together, they looked around the room, their minds as one, forming the same images.

He turned her to him and stroked her long hair away from her face and smiled tenderly.

'Have I ever told you how much I love you?' he asked softly.

'Every day.'

'So you won't mind hearing it again…'

'Nope.'

'I love you, Mrs Decroix.'

HARLEQUIN®
Presents

The world's bestselling romance series...
The series that brings you your favorite authors,
month after month:

Helen Bianchin...Emma Darcy
Lynne Graham...Penny Jordan
Miranda Lee...Sandra Marton
Anne Mather...Carole Mortimer
Susan Napier...Michelle Reid

and many more uniquely talented authors!

Wealthy, powerful, gorgeous men...
Women who have feelings just like your own...
The stories you love, set in exotic, glamorous locations...

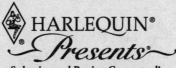

HARLEQUIN®
Presents

Seduction and Passion Guaranteed!

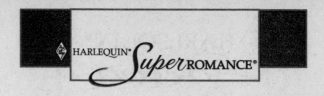

...there's more to the story!

Superromance.
A *big* satisfying read about unforgettable characters. Each month we offer *six* very different stories that range from family drama to adventure and mystery, from highly emotional stories to romantic comedies—and much more! Stories about people you'll believe in and care about. Stories too compelling to put down....

Our authors are among today's *best* romance writers. You'll find familiar names and talented newcomers. Many of them are award winners— and you'll see why!

If you want the biggest and best in romance fiction, you'll get it from Superromance!

Emotional, Exciting, Unexpected...

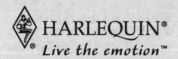

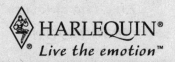

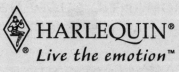

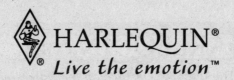

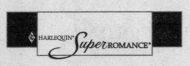

e◆HARLEQUIN.com

The Ultimate Destination for Women's Fiction

For FREE online reading, visit
www.eHarlequin.com now and enjoy:

Online Reads
Read **Daily** and **Weekly** chapters from
our Internet-exclusive stories by your
favorite authors.

Interactive Novels
Cast your vote to help decide how these
stories unfold...then stay tuned!

Quick Reads
For shorter romantic reads, try our
collection of Poems, Toasts, & More!

Online Read Library
Miss one of our online reads?
Come here to catch up!

Reading Groups
Discuss, share and rave with other
community members!

For great reading online,
visit www.eHarlequin.com today!